"Arlene?" She spoke as soon as the connection was made. "It's Mollie."

"Mollie! We've been calling you, but the line's been busy."

"Mom's been on the phone. Did you get it?"

"Uh-huh. I got Westside. How about you?"

"Vista," Mollie groaned. "What about Sandy?"

"She's going to Westside, too. I just talked to her."

"Oh, Arlene," Mollie wailed. "What am I going to do? How could this happen to me?"

"I heard my mom say the school board tried not to split up families; it's probably because of your sisters."

"Great," Mollie said. Her life would be ruined, just because of her two older sisters. "Do you think you could get your assignment switched?"

"You know what the letter said—no changes," the other girl answered. "Besides," she went on, her tone a bit dubious, "Jenny, Liz, and Michelle—it seems like everyone got Westside, Mollie."

"I think I'm going to die," Mollie groaned again, pulling a pillow over her face.

FAWCETT GIRLS ONLY BOOKS

SISTERS

THREE'S A CROWD #1

TOO LATE FOR LOVE #2

SISTERS

THREE'S A CROWD

Jennifer Cole

FAWCETT GIRLS ONLY • NEW YORK

A Fawcett Girls Only Book
Published by Ballantine Books
Copyright © 1986 by Cloverdale Press, Inc.

Library of Congress Catalog Card Number: 86-91086

ISBN 0-449-13004-5

Manufactured in the United States of America

First Edition: May 1986

Chapter 1

"*Alone!*" *The blue eyes of fourteen-year-old* Mollie Lewis widened, and she looked almost frightened.

"For ten days?" Cindy Lewis, fifteen, found that she was gaping like a fish, and quickly closed her mouth.

"Just the three of us?" Seventeen-year-old Nicole, the oldest of the three Lewis sisters, could hardly control her excitement.

"Slow down," their father told them, reaching for another slice of roast beef. "It's not settled yet; your mother and I are still discussing the idea."

"Yes," Mrs. Lewis agreed, her attention diverted as Mollie reached for the gravy. "Careful, Mollie. I think ten days is a long time to be gone, especially with school just about to start. And I'm not

sure I feel comfortable about leaving you girls alone."

"Mother!" Nicole sounded indignant. "You know I'm responsible. Everyone says so. Last year when my French teacher couldn't find a substitute, she let me teach the freshman class for a whole week."

"That was only for an hour a day," her father pointed out, his tone dry. But as he peered over his glasses, looking across the table at his three daughters, his gaze softened with pride and affection. Nicole, who resembled her mother, with her soft brown hair, slim figure, and even features, was pretty and graceful and, he had to admit, very responsible. Cindy, the tomboy of the trio, was athletically trim, tanned, and capable, with her short blond sunstreaked hair and green eyes. And Mollie, the baby, with her petite form already developing womanly curves, her softly waving blond hair and big blue eyes—how could a father not be proud of daughters such as these?

"It's not like we're babies or anything," Cindy interjected, not very pleased to see Nicole getting all of the credit for maturity. She wrinkled her nose at her father. "Why do you have to go to Japan, anyhow? I thought Mr. Shoemaker was making the trip." Adam Shoemaker was the senior partner of their father's architectural firm.

"Don't you remember? He had a heart attack a few days ago," Nicole reminded her younger sister. "How's he doing, Dad?"

"Much better; it was only a mild attack. But it definitely rules out a flight across the Pacific," their father told them. "And I thought this was too good an opportunity to miss—that's why I suggested to your mother that she come along. We can have a vacation after my seminars are completed."

"It would be wonderful, Richard." Mrs. Lewis's tone was wistful. "But the girls—"

"Oh, Mom!" Nicole protested. "You both said you wanted to take a trip alone as soon as you could, since you were too busy with the June wedding rush to get away for your twentieth anniversary. Now is the perfect time, before the holiday parties begin. *Mon Dieu,* this is the perfect opportunity!"

The three girls looked expectantly at their mother, waiting for her answer. Movable Feast, the catering business that Mrs. Lewis had started in their own kitchen, had long ago outgrown its modest beginnings, thanks to their mother's efficient management and talent. She now operated from a shop in town, and stayed as busy as she cared to be, often having to turn away business.

"That's true, Nicole," Laura Lewis agreed. "It does seem too good to pass up. I think I'll call your grandmother after dinner; maybe she can come stay."

Nicole's enthusiasm dimmed slightly. Fond as she was of her grandmother, if Gramma Lewis came to stay, then Nicole would not be the one in charge. And she rather liked that idea.

But nothing had been decided as yet. After they finished the fresh fruit dessert, Nicole jumped up. "Why don't you call now, Mother? We'll clear the table and clean up the kitchen."

"Why, that would be nice," Mrs. Lewis said, a bit startled by the unexpected offer.

Cindy swallowed her frown and waited until her parents had left the room before blurting out, "What's the big idea volunteering all of us? It's your night to clean up, Nicole!"

"Yes," Mollie agreed. "I'm expecting a call from Arlene."

"Then get busy and we'll get this done quickly. Use your heads, you ninnies." Nicole's tone sharpened. "We have to show Mom and Dad how well we can work together, or they'll never consider letting us stay by ourselves."

"But Gramma—" Mollie began, looking confused.

"Mother's calling her; that doesn't mean she's going to come. If we're lucky, she'll already have plans," Nicole informed them. "Now, hurry up. You two bring the dishes into the kitchen; I'll start with the pots and pans."

With all three of them working, the dishwasher was loaded, the counter and sink cleared, and the floor swept in no time.

"I need to call Arlene," Mollie still grumbled. "To see if she got her notice about school yet."

"That reminds me," Cindy exclaimed. "There's

a letter from the school board for Mom and Dad. I forgot to give it to them."

"What?" Mollie almost shrieked. "I checked the mailbox three times today. Why didn't you tell me?"

"You probably had your ear glued to the phone and didn't notice when I brought in the mail. Here it is. What are you squawking about? I'm telling you now, aren't I?"

"You two shut up!" Nicole sounded so fierce that Mollie bit back her angry rebuttal, grabbed the envelope, and turned toward the kitchen door just as their mother came into the room.

"You did a very good job, girls," their mother commented.

Nicole threw her two sisters a look that said "I told you so." Cindy grinned, but Mollie refused to acknowledge her oldest sister's foresight.

"Did you talk to Gramma?"

"Yes," Mrs. Lewis told them. "But she's in bed with the flu."

"Oh, wow." Cindy bit back her first words and she said instead, "That's awful."

Mrs. Lewis didn't seem to notice the quick change of emotion. "Yes, I'm sure she'll be fine soon. She can't come down. I tried to call Cousin Jenny, but she wasn't home. I'll try again tomorrow. Is something wrong, Mollie?"

Mollie, who had ripped open the white envelope and now stared fixedly at the letter inside, shook her head. She held out the form for her mother to read.

"You've been assigned to Vista High; that's a relief," Mrs. Lewis commented, scanning the letter quickly. "I was worried about this new school zoning. I certainly would hate to have you girls in different high schools."

Mollie nodded.

"Nicole, would you help me hem my new blue skirt? If we do go, I'd like to take the skirt along."

"Sure," Nicole said as she followed her mother out of the kitchen.

"What's the matter, Mollie?" Cindy asked, noticing the younger girl's glum expression. "Don't you want to go to Vista?"

"I guess so," Mollie answered slowly. "If Arlene and Sandy get Vista."

Cindy, knowing that Mollie's two best friends from junior high lived on the other side of the subdivision, shrugged. "They probably will."

"I hope so; I'll just die if they don't!"

Accustomed to her sister's theatrics, Cindy paid no attention. "If you're going to make a phone call, hurry up and do it. I want to call Anna and Duffy and see if they'll be at the beach tomorrow."

"They're always at the beach; why waste a phone call?" Mollie ran for the kitchen door, dodging the dish towel that Cindy snapped expertly at her little sister.

Mollie ran all the way up the carpeted stairs and removed the phone from the hall table. The

long extension cord her parents had added allowed the sisters to pull it into any of their rooms.
It barely reached Mollie's. Shutting the door behind her, she surveyed her bedroom, which was
in its usual state of chaos. One wall was neatly—
well, fairly neatly—covered in a bright floral print
that she had stapled to the wall herself, inspired
by a decorating article in last month's issue of
Seventeen. But something had interrupted her
project—she couldn't recall now whether it was
the boy who had been visiting across the street
or the summer talent show at the Y—and she'd
never finished the job. The other three walls were
plastered with a hodgepodge of Clark Gable, Matt
Dillon, and Mel Gibson posters. Her favorite was
of Scarlett O'Hara dancing in Rhett Butler's arms.
But just now Mollie ignored them all and quickly
dialed her best friend's number.

"Arlene?" She spoke as soon as the connection
was made. "It's Mollie."

"Mollie! We've been calling you, but the line's
been busy."

"Mom's been on the phone. Did you get it?"

"Uh-huh. I got Westside. How about you?"

"Vista," Mollie groaned. "What about Sandy?"

"She's going to Westside, too. I just talked to
her."

"Oh, Arlene," Mollie wailed. "What am I going
to do? How could this happen to me?"

"I heard my mom say that the school board

tried not to split up families; it's probably because of your sisters."

"Great," Mollie said. Her life would be ruined, just because of her two older sisters. "Do you think you could get your assignment switched?"

"You know what the letter said—no changes," the other girl answered. "Besides," she went on, her tone a bit dubious, "Jenny, Liz, and Michelle—it seems like everyone got Westside, Mollie."

"I think I'm going to die," Mollie groaned again, pulling a pillow over her face.

"Mollie? I can't hear you."

"Sorry." Mollie emerged from the ruffled pillowcase, and the two girls talked for a few more minutes. But after bewailing the unkind fate that had separated them, there didn't seem to be too much to say. After Mollie said good-bye and replaced the receiver, she curled up on her bed, completely overcome with misery.

All summer long Mollie had dreamed about her first year in high school. Junior high had been okay, but "high school" had a magic ring to it, as if her life were really beginning. But along with her rising anticipation had come an increasing nervousness. A whole new school, new classes, new teachers—new boys! Mollie was excited and anxious at the same time.

Now she was just anxious; she'd never expected to have to start her freshman year all alone! This change in the school zoning, due to overcrowding at Vista, seemed to Mollie a personal disaster.

She had coasted through junior high with friends she'd known for years. She knew that she was well liked—by both the girls and the boys, and not just because she was pretty. In fact, she'd had it fairly easy, and she'd never really thought about it until now, when all her security had suddenly been stripped away.

Start high school without any friends! Could there be anything more horrendous? So what if she had two older sisters at Vista? Big deal. Didn't the powers-that-be realize that she'd hardly see Cindy and Nicole in school? How could a sophomore and senior condescend to notice a mere freshman? Besides, none of their classes would be the same, so it hardly mattered. But to have Arlene and Sandy and all of her friends clear across town—Mollie groaned again and buried her head in the pillows.

She was hidden so deeply beneath the bed covering that she almost didn't hear the knock at the door. When it came again, Mollie lifted her head and called, "Who is it?"

"Just me," Cindy answered, pushing her portable stereo headphones temporarily off her ears and biting into one of several brownies she had piled onto a plate.

"Oh," Mollie sighed. She'd hoped it might be her mother, who usually noticed when something was wrong. "Come in."

Cindy walked in and perched on the edge of

the bed, holding out a brownie. "Are you still upset?"

The two sisters stared at each other: blue eyes locked with green. Mollie's wavy blond hair touched her shoulders as she tossed her head defiantly. Cindy stood there nonchalantly doing leg stretches while Mollie, her petite figure drawn up into a forlorn knot as she clasped her arms around her knees, felt tears welling up in her large dark blue eyes, eyes which had already entranced more male hearts than even Mollie had any idea of.

Mollie bristled at the casualness of the question as she pushed away the brownie. "Why shouldn't I be?" she demanded. "How would you feel if you'd just lost every friend you had and had to start a new school all alone?"

Cindy's expression sobered as she considered her sister's question. "You're right, shrimp. I'd be upset, too. But there's nothing you can do about it, far as I can see. Besides, you'll make lots of new friends."

"Easy for you to say," Mollie grumbled. "It's all your fault, anyhow."

"Me?" Cindy almost laughed at Molly's accusation, until she realized Mollie was serious. "What have I got to do with it?" she demanded as she pushed back her tousled blond hair, streaked from hours in the sun.

Mollie regarded her sister enviously as Cindy stretched her arms, which were rounded and firm from years of throwing a softball. Cindy never seemed to worry about anything, and she always looked completely at ease.

"If you and Nicole didn't go to Vista, I'd probably have been assigned to Westside like all my friends."

"You can hardly blame us for that." Cindy tried to be reasonable, but Mollie wasn't in the mood for logic.

"Want to bet?"

"Stay here and sulk, then." Cindy forgot that she had come upstairs intending to console her sister. Instead she bounded out of the room quickly, slamming the door behind her.

Mollie, alone once more, looked across the room at her half-open closet door. She and Arlene had already chosen similar outfits to wear on their first day of school. Now she might not even be wearing what the other freshmen did. And worse yet, who would she eat lunch with?

Mollie felt tears slide past her closed lids and touch her long lashes. All she could see ahead of her were problems. She pulled her quilt up to hide her face and wept in earnest.

When Cindy, clad in a paint-spattered sweat shirt and shorts, clattered down the steps early the next morning, singing along with her ever-present portable stereo, she was surprised to see Nicole standing over the stove, spatula in hand, watched closely by Winston, their always-hungry 150-pound black Newfoundland.

Beneath her apron, Nicole wore a soft blue blouse and a printed skirt with a feminine swirl of lace at the hem. As always, she looked feminine and tastefully pulled together. Her brown hair was pulled back in a smooth French braid, and her soft eyes were carefully, though subtly, made-up.

Cindy, who hadn't yet combed her hair and had already applied a layer of white sunblock to her nose, pulled off her headphones and stared.

"What are you up to now?" Although she knew that her older sister liked to cook, Nicole was hardly a morning person, and rarely made an appearance before ten-thirty in the morning during the summer.

"Making French toast."

"Of course. What else?" Cindy snickered. Nicole's predilection for all things French was already a family joke.

Nicole ignored her sister and replied patiently, "I told Mom I'd fix breakfast for you two. Is Mollie still asleep?"

"Probably in bed feeling sorry for herself." Cindy poured herself a glass of orange juice and came around to sit at the breakfast nook.

"What's the matter—no, don't tell me; she doesn't have a thing to wear."

"No, this is serious," Cindy acknowledged reluctantly. "She's been assigned to Vista."

"So?"

"But all her friends have been assigned to Westside," Cindy finished.

Even Nicole looked sober. "That's too bad. But she'll make more friends; Mollie's always been popular."

"Try convincing Mollie."

"Oh, no, this is terrible," Nicole worried. "If Mom finds out that Mollie's upset—"

"Wow," Cindy nodded, following her sister's train of thought. "Has Mom left yet?"

"No, she's upstairs," Nicole said. "We've got to keep Mollie out of sight until we can cheer her up."

As if on cue, the kitchen door swung open, and Mollie, wearing a bright green robe, walked into the room. For her to get up without being called was unusual in itself, but one glance at her pale face, swollen eyelids, and miserable expression was enough to tell anyone, especially their mother, that Mollie was pretty unhappy.

"What timing," Nicole muttered.

Mollie looked offended. "Do you want me to leave?"

"Yes!"

Nicole's answer was so emphatic that Mollie, already dejected, now appeared close to tears. "Thanks a lot."

"It's too late—here comes Mom!" Cindy hissed.

"Hurry, let's get her out of here." Nicole grabbed her younger sister and pushed her hastily toward the louvered doors of the big pantry.

"Hey!" Mollie protested. "What do you think you're doing?"

"Be quiet or you're dead!" Nicole commanded, then shut the door on her indignant sister.

"Everything all right, girls?" Laura Lewis, dressed in a neat beige skirt and cream-colored blouse, paused in the kitchen doorway. "I thought I heard Mollie."

"She's in the pantry, looking for some strawberry syrup," Nicole answered quickly.

Cindy watched in awe as her sister took command of the situation. "Awesome," she sputtered, trying to hide behind her glass of juice.

Fortunately, their mother seemed distracted and didn't detect the girls' tenseness. "Nicole, I need you to take care of things here today. I've an awful lot to do, getting ready for this trip, and I have to go by the shop, but I'll be home by dinner."

"We'll be fine," Nicole promised.

When they heard the car leave the garage, Nicole sighed in relief and she and Cindy both headed for the pantry.

They opened the door only to find Mollie sitting dejectedly on a large box of detergent. "Can I come out now?"

"Yes—oh, my toast is burning!" Nicole ran for the stove while Cindy grinned sheepishly at Mollie's injured expression.

"What's the big idea? Why was I shoved in the pantry?"

"Come on out, Mollie. Listen, I know you're unhappy about the school, but if Mom finds out that you're really upset, she might cancel her trip," Nicole said.

"So?"

Nicole shook her head. She could almost hear her sister thinking, Isn't that what mothers are for?

"Don't be so selfish," Nicole reasoned. "Mom's really excited about this trip; you should have heard her talking last night. She's always wanted to go to the Orient. And she and Dad haven't been on a vacation by themselves in ages; it'll be like a second honeymoon. Do you really want to spoil all that?"

Mollie looked sulky. "No."

"Then cheer up. What are you doing today?"

"Nothing."

"Well, don't sit around here and mope; you'll just get more depressed. Go to the beach with Cindy."

"Who said I wanted her?" Cindy demanded, then subsided beneath Nicole's glare. "Oh, all right."

"Who said I wanted to go?" Mollie retorted.

"Would you rather stay home and clean the house?" Nicole asked, her tone deceptively sweet. "I told Mom I'd get all the laundry done today."

"Get off it, Nicole," Cindy said. "I know you're trying to impress Mom and Dad, but if you keep up at this rate, they're bound to get suspicious!"

Mollie grinned for the first time, but Nicole ignored the quip. "Come eat breakfast," she said, stepping around Winston.

Everyone had a good day except Mollie. As she and Cindy pedaled away from their red-tiled, Spanish-style home, she couldn't even get excited about the prospect of a day at the beach. She didn't feel like joining her friends, who would all be talking about Westside. Not being a surfer like Cindy, she spent the entire day sunbathing and, still absorbed in her troubles, forgot to apply suntan lotion.

"At least she doesn't look pale anymore," Cindy pointed out when Nicole groaned at the sight of a lobster-red Mollie.

Mollie, steeped in sunburn ointment, made a heroic attempt at dinner and managed to hide her depression, which at least brought her back into her sisters' good graces. After dinner their mother went back to the telephone.

The three girls were in the family room in front of the TV when both their parents came into the room.

"I talk to Jenny, but she's about to leave on a cruise to Mexico," Mrs. Lewis told them.

"So?" Nicole held her breath, and Cindy and Mollie waited expectantly.

"So your father and I have talked it over, and we've decided that you're responsible enough to stay on your own. Your dad thinks it will be a good experience for you. I hope he's right." She smiled.

"Awesome!" Cindy blurted as she let out an excited whoop.

"Oh, Mom." Nicole bounded up and gave her mother an impulsive hug. "You won't be sorry. I promise! We'll be so good."

"Don't get too angelic; we want to recognize you girls when we get home." Mr. Lewis laughed.

Later, as the three sisters went up the staircase, Nicole said, "This is great. Just think—ten whole days by ourselves."

"That's the truth." Cindy grinned, thinking of long afternoons at the beach with no one to remind her of household chores.

"I hope so," Mollie sighed.

Chapter 2

*T*he next few days passed very quickly, with all the cleaning, packing, and last-minute instructions that their mother continued to issue. She tacked a list of important reminders to the bulletin board in the kitchen, along with a copy of the Lewises' itinerary and anything else that the girls might need. Before the girls knew it, it was Wednesday, the first day of school, and the day of their parents' departure.

"The phones all have emergency numbers taped to the side," Mrs. Lewis told them for what seemed like the twentieth time as Mr. Lewis carried out the last of the suitcases. The girls gathered around their mother for one last hug and kiss.

"Have fun, Mother," Nicole told her. "It should be so exciting." Not that Japan was quite as thrilling as France, she thought privately. But she didn't put her thoughts into words.

"We'll be fine," Cindy said. "Don't worry about a thing."

"Right," Mollie echoed, and smiled brightly, trying not to reveal her still very pressing anxieties.

"Just be careful, girls," Mrs. Lewis repeated.

"They'll be fine," her husband interrupted, holding the car door open for her. "I have all the faith in the world in you," Mr. Lewis told his daughters, slightly spoiling the effect by adding, "And if you need anything, go next door to the Robinsons."

"Right," the girls chorused. They gathered around their father for a quick hug. Then the car door slammed, and they watched the blue sedan pull out of the driveway and turn into the street.

Mollie, watched the car disappear from view, was conscious of a distinct emptiness in the pit of her stomach. But her sisters seemed so carefree and at ease, she wouldn't admit to her apprehension.

"Okay." Nicole spoke briefly, quickly taking charge. "I'll make breakfast. You two get dressed and make your beds."

"Make our beds? What difference does it make?" Cindy protested. "Nobody's here to see them."

"That's not the point." Nicole's tone was firm.

"Let's not get carried away with this older-sister-in-charge business," Cindy muttered under her breath. She and Mollie went back upstairs while Nicole, humming a French folk song, went to work in the kitchen.

By the time the younger girls came back down,

there were plates of fluffy scrambled eggs and crisp bacon sitting on the breakfast table. Nicole did have *some* good points, Cindy acknowledged in the back of her mind.

"Hurry up," Nicole ordered, not knowing that she was destroying Cindy's momentary goodwill. "You don't want to be late the first day of school."

"Hey, I'm always on time," Cindy protested. "Mollie's the one who can't get out of bed."

"That's not true!"

"It's twenty-five till eight." Nicole's tone was ominous.

"Drat!" Cindy choked down one more bite, then ran for her notebooks.

"Hey, wait for me," Mollie called, feeling a rush of nervousness threaten to overwhelm her. She paused in the hallway to peer into the oval mirror. Was she wearing the right sort of clothes? All of a sudden her black-and-yellow polka-dotted sundress seemed all wrong. She was sure it made her look like a bumblebee. She sighed, wishing she were taller and not quite so curvy. Her stomach felt as if it were a trampoline for a troupe of acrobats.

"What about you?" Cindy asked Nicole as she headed for the garage and her bike.

"Mark's picking me up." Nicole sounded smug.

Cindy stuck out her tongue, then ran for the back door. "Come on, Mollie, stop admiring yourself," she called.

The youngest Lewis came slowly through the doorway and pulled out her bike.

"Hurry up." Irritated by Mollie's dawdling, Cindy wheeled her bike toward the street. Mollie was forced to run after her.

"Cindy!" Mollie panted as she pedaled hard to catch up with her athletic sister. "Wait up."

"Start pedaling, then. I want to meet Anna before the bell rings."

They pedaled hard for a few minutes, with no breath to spare for talking. All the questions Mollie wanted to ask seemed stuck in her throat as she struggled to keep up with Cindy's pace. But her stomach still held that hollowness that seemed big enough to swallow an ocean. And when they saw the school building ahead, Mollie felt a wave of real panic.

"Cindy," she cried as they turned toward the bike racks. "I don't know where to go!"

"Relax, shrimp." Cindy looked around, seeming to detect her sister's fear for the first time. "All the freshmen will meet in the gym. You'll get a pep talk, and they'll give you your schedule."

"But I don't know where anything is. I'll get lost," Mollie moaned.

"Calm down. You'll find your classrooms. Everyone's lost the first day," Cindy told her, and then peered closely at her for the first time that morning. "Hey, have you got a black eye?"

"Do I?" Molly shrieked, pulling out a mirror. "Oh, that's my eye makeup." Mollie sounded insulted. "I didn't want to look like a little kid today!"

"Great, you look like a raccoon instead. Come on, I'll walk you to the gym. Hey, there's Anna." Cindy spotted her tall, dark-haired friend across the lawn.

As Cindy called to Anna, Mollie gulped hard, thankful for any support, although she felt Cindy could be a little nicer. While Cindy and Anna talked, Mollie followed meekly behind them, wishing for just a fraction of her sister's easy assurance and, gazing enviously at Anne, just a fraction of Anna's height. The three paused at the entrance to the gym, and Mollie stared at the sight of the milling students within the double doors. What a crowd of strange faces! Oh, help! Mollie thought wildly.

"Go on in. The bell's about to ring," Cindy told her, giving her a shove through the doors. "You'll be okay. See you this afternoon."

Mollie, looking very pale, walked inside.

"She doesn't look so good," Anna commented. "You don't think she's going to throw up or something, do you?"

"Mollie's the nervous type," Cindy said. "She always overreacts. In an hour or two, she'll be fine."

"I guess so." Anna threw one last glance toward the gym, then the two girls headed for their lockers. They had taken only a few steps when they almost fell over a boy who had stooped to tie his shoelaces.

"Hey, Jimmy, what's the big idea?" Cindy demanded.

"Sorry." The boy reached for his notebooks, and something moved inside the pocket of his sweat shirt.

"What's that?" Anna gasped.

"Just this guy." Jimmy pulled out an enormous green frog, who stared back at the girls with large bulging eyes.

"What's that for—your favorite teacher?" Cindy joked.

"No, I found him on the road; I thought I'd give him to the biology teacher," the boy told them.

"Ugh!" Anna groaned, and even Cindy appeared daunted. "Don't do that. He'll dissect him," she argued. "That would be awful. That frog is enjoying life; just look at him."

They all stared at the large frog, who croaked loudly. Anna jumped.

"What should I do, then?" Jimmy asked. "I've got to go to history, and if Mrs. Smith sees him, she'll kill me."

"Give him to me; I'll let him go in the park," Cindy offered.

Jimmy handed over the large frog, and Cindy held him gingerly by one hand.

"What are you going to do with him in the meantime?" Anna couldn't decide whether to laugh or groan.

"I'll put him in my lunchbag."

"With your sandwich?"

"Well, no," Cindy agreed. "Here, put my food in your bag."

When the frog was safely enveloped inside the brown bag, they headed once more toward their lockers.

"We're going to be late," Anna warned.

"Relax; nobody's on time the first day of school. You sound just like Nicole."

"Is that bad?"

"She's being a real pain," Cindy confessed. "This business of being in charge is going to her head."

Just then another familiar face appeared in the crowd of students, and Cindy forgot her complaints. "Look, there's Duffy."

She waved toward the tall, redheaded boy. "Hey, Duffy, where's your first class?"

"In the north wing." Despite his statement, Duffy seemed disposed to linger in front of one of the typing rooms.

"So what are you hanging around here for?" Anna asked bluntly. "And what's that under your arm?"

Cindy noticed for the first time the pink knapsack with the designer logo. "Duff, is that yours?"

Duffy's good-natured face reddened. "It's Mary Ann's. She left it at my house yesterday; I'm just returning it."

"Mary Ann?" Cindy's enthusiasm took a nosedive, and Anna sniffed. "That dippy girl in last year's English class, who screamed about everything?"

"She's not dippy!" Duffy sounded angry.

"Okay, already," Cindy told him, thinking, How could a nice guy like Duffy go mushy over an airhead? Growing four inches over the summer obviously wasn't the only way her surfing buddy had changed.

"So give it to her." Anna seemed offended.

"I meant to, but she's surrounded by a bunch of girls, and I ... I don't want it to look like ... you know." Duffy stared down at his tennis shoes.

"Would you like me to give it to her for you?" Cindy asked.

Anna stared at her friend, suspicious over this sudden change of tone.

"I'll tell her you're returning it."

"Would you?" Duffy brightened at once. "Thanks, Cindy. See you at polo practice tomorrow." He handed over the pink knapsack and made tracks for the other end of the school.

"Why are you being so sweet all of a sudden?" Anna demanded as she watched Cindy unzip the knapsack.

"I'm going to give Mary Ann a little excitement." Cindy grinned.

"You wouldn't!" Anna gasped as Cindy reached inside her lunchbag for the wiggling frog.

"Want to bet?" With the frog neatly inserted inside the knapsack, Cindy carefully zipped the top.

"Duffy's going to *kill* you," Anna warned, giggling despite her warning.

"I know." Cindy grinned. She walked over to the doorway, peering into the crowd of students.

"Hey, Mary Ann," Cindy called. "Over here."

A short brunette separated herself from a clump of girls and came closer to the door. "What is it?"

"I have something for you, from Duffy."

"Oh." Mary Ann nodded and reached for the knapsack. "I wondered where I'd left that. Duffy's a real doll."

Cindy grimaced as she slipped quietly away with Anna close behind her.

"Cindy . . . you're really something!" Anna's tone held both admiration and apprehension. "What will she do when—"

A sudden high-pitched shriek rose from the room behind them, followed by a chorus of minor squeals.

Cindy started to laugh. "Let's get out of here," she urged. The girls began to run.

Nicole was waiting on the front step when Mark pulled up in his battered Chevy. Smiling as she ran forward, she greeted him with a light kiss, affectionately touching his curly brown hair. Mark had been away for the weekend with his parents, and she hadn't had a chance to tell him the big news.

"Guess what," she said as she shut the car door

behind her. "My parents have gone to Japan for ten days."

"Who's staying over, your grandmother?"

"No," Nicole proudly told him. "I'm in charge."

"Just you girls—great!"

"Isn't it? Just think: We can have the house to ourselves—and no curfew." Nicole sighed.

"But there are your sisters to consider," Mark pointed out.

"We can watch a late movie, listen to music, all in privacy," she continued.

"With your sisters," Mark reminded her.

"I could cook a romantic dinner for just the two of us," Nicole added.

Mark squeezed her hand. "That's a great idea. Course, we'll be stuck with your kid sisters, so it won't be all fun and games."

"Oh, they won't be a problem," Nicole promised.

"You don't think so?" Mark sounded less certain. "I had to watch my two nephews one weekend, and it was pure misery. The things those kids could get into."

"Cindy and Mollie aren't like that," Nicole assured him. "We won't have any trouble." But Nicole felt a moment of unease when she recalled Mollie's pale face that morning. Should she have paid more attention to Mollie's freshman fears? She pushed the thought away. Knowing Mollie, she was probably feeling better already.

As they drove into the school parking lot, Nicole glanced at her watch and exclaimed, "I've got to run. I can't be late for French. *Au revoir.*"

Mark, accustomed to Nicole's French mania, grinned.

Nicole made it to the familiar French classroom, with its bulletin boards covered with French posters and maps, before the first bell.

"*Bonjour,* Madame Preston," she called merrily to the gray-haired woman behind the large desk.

"Ah, *ma chère* Nicole," the teacher replied, smiling at one of her favorite pupils. They chatted briskly in French for a few moments, then Nicole took her seat.

None of the other students had been in her class last year, but she noticed one new student, whose sleekly cut brunette hair and all-black outfit adorned with large pieces of silver jewelry drew more than one stare from the other kids.

The new girl was introduced to the class as Angela Coulter, a transfer student from Long Island. While the whole class stared at the attractive dark-haired girl with interest, Nicole, listening to Angela's fluent French as she answered the teacher's questions, felt a strong wave of admiration. What an interesting girl!

When the hour ended, Nicole made a point of waiting at the side of the room so that she could speak to the new girl. Several other classmates spoke to Nicole as they passed—she had always been well liked in school—but Nicole waited patiently until Angela approached the doorway.

"Hi, my name's Nicole Lewis. How do you like Santa Barbara so far?"

"A bit raw around the edges," the other girl answered, her tone cool. "But I suppose I'll adjust."

"I guess you miss the East Coast." Nicole, a little startled by this chilly response, almost faltered. "Really, there are lots of things to do—"

"Perhaps." Angela looked her up and down in an appraising manner.

Nicole, who knew that her outfit was attractive and fashionable, still wanted to glance down at her linen skirt and lilac silk blouse to see if she would pass muster.

But apparently she did, because the girl's expression softened, and she went on with slightly more warmth. "It hardly matters; as soon as this year is over, I'm going back east to attend Vassar, then probably on to Paris."

"Really?" Nicole's enthusiasm returned. "I'm planning to attend my junior year in Paris, and I want to do graduate work at the Sorbonne. I want to study art history."

"I spent last summer in Paris with my stepmother," Angela told her.

"How exciting!" Nicole followed Angela into the hallway. "I'd love to hear about the Paris fashions."

"Come down to my locker. I've got a few magazines I bought in Paris."

"Terrific ... oh." Nicole hesitated, seeing a familiar face coming down the hallway.

"What is it?"

"My little sister, Mollie. I meant to wait and talk to her; she has French One in this classroom next hour. I wanted to see how she is. She was awfully nervous this morning," Nicole explained.

The other girl shrugged, her boredom obvious. "Well, if you need to baby-sit, maybe I'll catch you later in the day."

"No, wait." Nicole, hoping to make a lunch date with Angela, felt torn. She threw another glance toward Mollie and tried to convince herself that Mollie's expression was less glum than it had been earlier. "I'll go with you. I'm sure Mollie is okay." They both strolled down the hall without another backward look.

Chapter 3

*M*ollie couldn't remember a time when she had been less okay. It began with the freshman assembly in the gym. The sea of strange faces made her stomach quiver. She slipped inside the double doors and glanced around, hoping for a familiar face. Her heart seemed to be beating so hard that Mollie thought she must be trembling all over.

Then, across the room, Mollie glimpsed a girl she had known in junior high—not one of her closest friends, but Janet at least wasn't a stranger. Heartened, Mollie tried to push through the milling students toward the far side of the large room.

"Would everyone be seated, please," a male voice boomed over a loudspeaker.

The students began to search for places to sit. Long rows of folding chairs had been arranged along the gym floor.

"Be seated, please," the ominous voice over the loudspeaker repeated.

Mollie, caught in a group of strangers, was forced to take the closest empty chair. She didn't want to be the last person standing—how embarrassing!

She had lost sight of Janet, and while the assistant principal began his welcoming speech, Mollie plunged into new depths of despair. The whole world was against her!

After all the instructions had been given—most of which Mollie was too dejected to remember—the students were directed toward the end of the gym. Several tables were set up to distribute schedules, and a large diagram of the school was posted on the wall to help the new students.

Mollie dutifully stood in the G–L line and eventually was handed her updated schedule. She glanced over the printout without interest. After all the disasters that had already befallen her, what else could happen?

Most of the subjects were identical to the sample schedule she had filled out last spring. Freshman English, Algebra I, French I, physical science. She had requested drama, having loved her experiences in the junior high plays, but she saw now that she had been placed in Speech I instead. That figured. It was her day for bad luck.

Her first class was algebra. Mollie looked over the school diagram, located the room number, and headed toward the hallway.

As Mollie hurried along, she was comforted just

a little to see other freshmen consulting their slips of paper, peering anxiously at room numbers, and generally—just as Cindy had predicted—looking as confused as Mollie herself.

Fortunately, she found the algebra room without any trouble and was able to slip into one of the rear desks just as the bell rang.

The teacher, a tiny, brisk woman with a no-nonsense attitude, hardly waited for the sharp twang of the bell to fade before she introduced herself and began handing out thick packets of papers.

"This is a pretest, students," the teacher announced. "No grade, so there's no reason to worry. I simply want to see how adequate your preparation in math has been and how much you've forgotten over the summer."

Mollie glanced over the pages she was given, and her heart sank. Math had never been one of her best subjects, and while some of the problems were familiar, quite a few looked like the product of a bad dream. Horrified, she wondered if she had ever studied this stuff.

The hour passed quickly. All the students labored over the pretest, and if Mollie hadn't been so preoccupied with her own worries, she might have noticed that many of the other freshmen looked just as bewildered as she felt. By the time the bell signaled the end of the class, the papers had been collected and textbooks assigned, and Mollie left the classroom with the terrible conviction that she was obviously too dumb to ever comprehend higher mathematics.

A failure the first day—and a failure with no friends. Mollie swallowed hard and began to search for her next class.

As she neared the French classroom, Mollie's mood lifted when she glimpsed a face she knew. Nicole was in the hallway talking to a tall brunette girl wearing a rather exotic outfit. Hoping to catch her sister's eye, Mollie hurried toward them. Even talking to an older sister would make her feel less lonely.

But to Mollie's disappointment, Nicole moved on down the hall before she was close enough to speak to her.

Feeling pretty low, Mollie went into the classroom. Looking around the room, she noticed several students gathered around a tall, thin brunette who appeared to be recounting the plot of last night's episode of a popular situation comedy. The girl gestured as she spoke, and her eyes were alight with intelligence and humor. Mollie, drawn toward her, came closer.

"Go on, Sarah," a blond girl encouraged.

"—And then she said, 'My cousin only ... only ...' Oh darn, I've forgotten the punch line."

Without thinking, Mollie picked up where the girl had left off, not only finishing the line but interjecting all of her instinctive talent for mimicry. "She said, 'My cousin only eats dead chickens.' "

All the kids laughed, but the tall girl looked

startled, and not too pleased. Before Mollie had a chance to speak to her, a slightly chunky dark-haired boy claimed her attention.

"You're pretty funny; what's your name?"

"Mollie Lewis."

"Here, sit down. Bell's about to ring." He practically propelled Mollie into the desk next to his.

Mollie, glancing back toward the girl she had hoped to meet, saw the girl watching them with a hostile expression. Maybe she shouldn't have stolen her audience, Mollie realized belatedly. Maybe she thought Molly was only trying to show off and didn't realize that she was trying to join the group.... Nothing was going right today.

"Bonjour," the gray-haired, slightly plump woman said, flashing an attractive smile. *"Je suis* Madame Preston. I'm very happy to see you all in French One, and I think we should take a few minutes to get acquainted. I want each of you to introduce yourself—in French, of course."

A slight ripple of laughter rose from the seated students, and Mollie found some of her gloom lifting.

"You will say, *'Bonjour, je m'appelle*—your name—' then tell us briefly a little about yourself. Later we will try to speak as much French as possible, but I realize there are limits to what we can do the first day"—more laughter from the class—"so the rest of your comments may be given in English."

At least this teacher was reasonable, Mollie

thought. She waited in interest as the first girl in the front stood up.

"*Bonjour, je m'appelle* Sandra Wallis; my hobbies are scuba diving and marine biology, and I'm on the school swim team."

Mollie cringed and thought, What on earth am I going to say—"I like to read teen magazines, watch the latest videos, and go shopping"? The class would never be impressed by that. Mollie's ambitions varied from week to week, and she didn't do anything special. What could she say? she thought wildly.

The second student in the row was a boy. He stood and faced the class. "*Je m'appelle* Alex. My father is a banker; we lived two years in Switzerland. I won second place in the district track meet last year."

Worse and worse. Mollie wanted to sink down in her desk. What was she going to say that could possibly impress these kids? If only she were Nicole . . .

Then it was her turn, and she forced her suddenly wobbly knees to push her upward. The whole group of faces turned toward her.

Panic-stricken, Mollie's mind raced. She would *be* Nicole. Drawing upon all her innate acting ability, Mollie drew herself up very straight and tried to sound as poised and sophisticated as her older sister. "*Je m'appelle* Mollie Lewis. My interests are art, especially French Impressionism, and interior design. I intend to study in Paris someday."

The students around her looked suitably impressed, but Mollie sank back into her seat, feeling like a fraud. Too late she detected a quizzical gleam in the teacher's eye, and remembered that Mrs. Preston knew Nicole quite well. Blushing—did the instructor realize that she had "borrowed" her sister's interests and ambitions?—Mollie stared down at her desk and hardly noticed the rest of the class go through their introductions.

Not until Mrs. Preston began to call students up to her desk to pass out textbooks did Mollie look around at the other students once more. The two girls she had noticed earlier, the plump blonde in the blue cotton sweater, and Sarah, the tall brunette, were whispering to each other. Mollie wished she could be part of their group.

When a likely moment came, Mollie smiled at them, hoping they would say something friendly. But they appeared to be ignoring her. Meanwhile, the boy behind her kept poking Mollie in the shoulder, forcing her to turn and listen to his childish comments.

"Want to see my sports magazine?"

"I wish there were some human beings in this class!" Mollie snapped, her patience gone.

Sarah had obviously overheard her, and her expression became more hostile than ever as she frowned and looked at Mollie—but this time Mollie was happy to ignore her.

When it was Mollie's turn to go up to receive a

textbook, she approached the front of the room with reluctance.

"Mollie Lewis? Are you Nicole's sister?"

Mollie nodded, dreading the teacher's next comment, but the woman only said, "I thought so. Nice to have you in French One, Mollie. I hope you continue to be interested in French art."

Mollie smiled weakly, then picked up her textbook and hurried back to her desk. *Does she know I made all that up?* Mollie wondered.

Once again, she was glad when the period ended. Not wanting to encounter Sarah and her friend, she waited until most of the other students, including the dark-haired boy who seemed to have a ten-year-old mentality, had left the classroom, then followed the crowd slowly into the hall.

The whole walkway was filled with milling, talking students. Mollie felt as if she stood out like a single black ant alone in a swarm of red ants. Everyone seemed to have someone to talk to— except her.

Suddenly, through a gap in the crowd she saw the girl she had glimpsed during the morning assembly.

"Janet?" Mollie darted through a throng of boys and grabbed the other girl's arm. The plump girl stared at her in surprise.

"Oh, Mollie."

"What do you think of high school—pretty nerve-racking, isn't it?" Mollie said. "What's your schedule like?" She knew she was babbling, but the relief of finding someone she knew was overwhelming.

"Not bad."

"Want to eat lunch together?" Mollie hoped for a positive answer. Facing a whole cafeteria alone would be the last straw.

But Janet only shrugged. "I don't know. I'm supposed to meet my cousin and her friends; maybe I'll see you there."

"Sure." Mollie's happiness evaporated as quickly as it had come. Everyone had friends already, except her.

"Isn't Arlene with you?" Janet asked.

"She got sent to Westside," Mollie explained dully.

"Oh, too bad. I'd better go. See you around."

"Yeah."

Mollie leaned against a row of lockers, feeling like the world's biggest reject. What had happened to her—instant unpopularity? When she looked up, she saw that the hall was almost empty. Better get to class.

But the question was, which class? Mollie couldn't remember where she was supposed to be. Where was her schedule?

Searching frantically through her notebook, Mollie scrambled through notes and homework assignments. Then she looked up and down the hall, but all the doors looked alike.

When the bell sounded its vibrant peal, Mollie realized she was quite alone and began to breathe quickly. She was late—and she didn't even know to what.

The sound of footsteps made her look up. A very tall, stern-looking man frowned down at her.

"Where are you supposed to be, young lady?"

"I ... I don't know!" Mollie wailed, feeling the prickling of tears behind her long lashes. How humiliating!

As she tried to gulp back her tears, the man seemed to relent, and said more mildly, "You must be a freshman. Don't you have a schedule?"

"I did, but I can't find it!" Mollie felt very foolish. She could picture herself wandering around school for the rest of the week; everyone would hear about the freshman who was too dumb to know her own schedule. Talk about embarrassment!

"You'd better come down to the office and let them make out another copy," the man was saying, but as Mollie shifted the books in her arms, a slip of paper suddenly fluttered toward the floor.

Mollie grabbed the errant slip. "That's it!"

The teacher smiled. "Better run, then. You're late already."

Mollie did as he suggested. Not until she rounded the corner did she pause to catch her breath and check for room numbers. When she finally found the right door, she slipped inside self-consciously, aware of the teacher's glance, and sat down in the back of the room. Then she copied her schedule down in three different places in her notebooks.

When lunchtime came, Mollie seriously considered skipping the whole thing, but she didn't know where else to go. For a minute she considered hiding in the bathroom—but that was ridiculous. The large cafeteria full of laughing students was so intimidating that she hovered at the back of the room, pretending to study a bulletin board of student activities, unwilling to face the long line of students waiting to buy food.

Someone clapped her on the shoulder, and Mollie jumped.

"How's it going, shrimp?"

"Oh, Cindy," Mollie exclaimed. "It's terrible!"

"That bad? Didn't you bring a lunch?"

"I forgot to pack one. I meant school. Anyhow, I'm not hungry."

Mollie followed Cindy and Anna to a table and sat down beside her sister. "I've only seen one girl I know, and she wasn't exactly excited to see me. And the other kids are so ... so ..."

"Give it time," Cindy advised, biting into her sandwich and greeting some more of her friends. "You'll meet some people, and make lots of friends."

"I doubt it." Watching Cindy eat made Mollie aware of the emptiness in her stomach, and she reached for one of her sister's cookies. "It's going to be a terrible year."

"It'll get better," Cindy promised, watching in resignation as her sister ate the rest of her lunch. "Like some milk with that?"

"No, thanks," Mollie said. "They don't like me, Cindy."

"Why not? You're crazy." Cindy's frown was perplexed. "You're a nice kid."

Mollie, remembering her pretensions in French class and the nasty crack that Sarah had overheard, spoke glumly. "Am I?"

Just then Cindy's friend Carey approached with a boy who stopped at their table and grinned at Cindy. "Duffy's looking for you, Lewis; says he's going to take you apart at the seams."

"Whoops. I think it's time to leave. See you this afternoon, Mollie."

"Sure." Mollie watched as Cindy and the other three left the room together. That was all she wanted—friends. Left by herself at a table filled with kids she didn't know, Mollie blushed and stared down at Cindy's leftover lunch.

The afternoon was no better than the morning, and by the time Mollie came to her last class, she only wanted this awful day to be over. When the teacher, a young woman, began to go over her list of students, she didn't seem to have Mollie's name.

"Maybe I'm in the wrong class." Molly felt a surge of hope. "I wanted to take drama."

"No, here you are," Mrs. Foster told her. "Speech One is a prerequisite for drama; you can take that next year. If you're interested, we'll be having open tryouts for our first student production in a few weeks."

"That would be great—I acted in all the junior high plays," Molly told her, happy for the first time that day. Then she saw several students watching her, and bit her lip. She didn't want to sound like she was showing off again. She opened her notebook.

"So, you're an actress," a male voice said from behind her.

Looking around in surprise, Mollie saw a good-looking boy with a magnetic smile and wavy blond hair. He was smiling—at her!

"I . . . I don't know," she stammered. "I mean, yes, I want to be. That's why I wanted to take drama; I didn't know freshmen couldn't enroll."

"You won't be a freshman forever," the boy pointed out, with such an air of authority that the simple statement seemed to express great wisdom.

"That's true," Mollie agreed. "And it's probably the nicest thought I've had today!" Some of her usual effervescence returned. "Maybe we'll survive."

"We?"

Mollie felt confused. "Aren't you a freshman?"

"Don't insult me! I'm a senior."

"Oh, I'm sorry," Mollie stammered again, sure that she'd offended him. Then, when his lips relaxed into a wide grin, she realized that he'd been teasing her, and she smiled, too.

"My name's Brett Harrington."

"Mollie Lewis," Mollie told him, thinking how amazingly good-looking he was. What luck to find him seated right behind her. "What are you doing in Speech?"

"I wanted an easy class—they only permit so many study halls," Brett confessed. "All you have to do in this class is talk, more or less, and I can always talk."

Mollie laughed, thrilled that someone "normal" was at last paying attention to her.

"Are you going to try out for the play?" he asked.

"I think so," Mollie told him.

"If you do, I might try out myself and see how it feels to be in the spotlight."

"You'd be a natural," Mollie predicted, hoping that he couldn't tell how impressed she was. She dipped her long lashes briefly and was sure he smiled even more broadly.

"We don't have to wait till then to get together. How about a Coke after school?"

Things were moving along a little rapidly for Mollie. She wondered what Nicole would say about a good-looking senior paying attention to her little sister. A lot, probably.

"Not today," she told him, smiling sweetly to take the sting out of her rejection. "I'm sort of tied up. Maybe later."

"Sure."

Then the teacher called the class to order, and Mollie had to turn back to face the front of the room.

But the heavy weight of despair that had threatened to totally ruin her freshman debut had lifted, and for the first time Mollie had something to smile about.

Chapter 4

*A*fter school Mollie got to the bike rack first, so she waited for her sister. Watching groups of students wander out of the school, Mollie again felt her keen sense of loneliness. When Cindy and Anna finally appeared, laughing and talking, Mollie's loneliness only increased.

"How'd it go, shrimp?" Cindy finally thought to ask, after they had unchained their bikes and rolled them away from the rack.

"Terrible." Mollie's tone was heavy with despair. "It was the worst day of my entire life!"

Anna looked suitably impressed, but Cindy, accustomed to Mollie's tendency to exaggerate, merely shrugged. "It'll get better. Come on." She began to pedal.

Mollie climbed hastily onto her bike, disappointed in Cindy's response, and followed the other two girls down the street. Big help you are, she thought, looking forward to pouring out her woes to her mother. Then she remembered her parents wouldn't be home for almost two weeks. Nobody was here to take her side! Life was rotten.

By the time she and Cindy reached home, Mollie felt as if no one in the world cared about her. When she walked into the kitchen and saw Nicole mixing something in a bowl, she refused to smile at her sister.

"How was school?"

Nicole sounded interested, but Mollie, remembering how Nicole hadn't waited for her after French, wouldn't be placated.

"A disaster!" she snapped, and continued toward her room.

Nicole, puzzled and a little miffed, turned to Cindy, who was opening the refrigerator. "What's with her?"

"Oh, a bad case of freshman blues," Cindy said cheerfully as she reached for the last piece of barbecued chicken. "You know Mollie. She'll be a different person by tomorrow."

"I hope so." Nicole felt slightly guilty. She should have taken the time at school to check on Mollie, try to cheer her up. What were sisters for, if not to stick together when things were rough? But on the other hand, Mollie could make a big deal out of nothing. Nicole looked down at her mixing bowl. After all, she was busy taking care of them. What did Mollie expect, anyway?

Mollie, who had dropped her books on her

desk and curled up in the middle of her unmade bed, was unaware of her older sister's conflict. All she knew was that high school was terrible; the girls were aloof and unfriendly, and her own sisters weren't much better. The memory of Brett's wide smile cheered her for a moment, but even that brief euphoria soon faded, and Mollie's depression returned.

The slight impact of a small body on the bed made Molly look up. It was the younger of their two cats, Cinders. A long-legged, still-gawky youngster with mottled gray fur, he walked across the tumbled bedcovers to rub his head against her shoulder.

She rubbed his soft fur and scratched behind his ears. The cat began to purr, a soft, vibrant sound that lifted Mollie's spirits just slightly. "At least you care about me," she told the cat.

A slight sound made Mollie look up; Nicole stood in the doorway.

"Dinner's ready," her sister said. Her friendly expression—she had come upstairs intending to chat with Mollie and try to discover why she was so unhappy with school—changed to annoyance as she looked into the room. "*Mon Dieu!* This is a pigsty. You didn't even make your bed."

"What difference does it make?" Mollie demanded.

"Make that bed up right now and get downstairs before my soufflé falls!" Nicole disappeared from sight.

Grumbling beneath her breath, Mollie pushed the cat gently off the bed, pulled the top cover over the tangled sheets, and headed for the stairs. "Some people," she told Cinders, who followed her down the steps, "let authority go to their heads."

"What did you say?" Cindy asked from behind her.

"Nothing."

In the kitchen the breakfast table was set with brightly colored place mats and a rose in a bud vase.

"Trying to win a prize from *Good Housekeeping*?" Cindy asked Nicole.

"There's no need not to do things right just because Mom and Dad are gone." Nicole's tone was lofty.

"Yes, Madam Etiquette." Cindy made a mock bow, and Nicole frowned at her.

"Hurry up; my soufflé's going to fall. Did you wash your hands?"

"Yes, right after watching *Sesame Street*," Cindy retorted. "Cut it out, Nicole. You're treating us like we're three years old."

Nicole dished up the soufflé in dignified silence.

Mollie only poked her fork into the food on her plate, sighing, "I'd rather have had a hamburger. What's this green stuff?"

Nicole looked insulted. "This is one of my best recipes. It's delicious; eat!"

Mollie didn't appear convinced. "What's in it?"

Even Cindy put down her fork, forcing Nicole to answer.

"It's a spinach soufflé."

Mollie wailed, "You know I hate spinach!"

"You haven't even tasted it!" Nicole's voice rose, but Mollie's lower lip set stubbornly. Nicole's feeling of being in control of the situation was disappearing quickly.

"I'm going to make myself a peanut butter sandwich."

"Do what you want—" Nicole began, when they all started at the thumping sound coming from the end of the kitchen. The girls turned to look. Winston, the big Newfoundland, was pushing his plastic food dish across the floor with his nose. The dish was empty.

"Cindy." Nicole's tone was sharp. "It was your turn to feed the animals."

"How can you sit there eating knowing that Winston is hungry?" Mollie demanded.

Cindy, who had already risen from the table, flashed her an angry look.

"And don't forget the cats," Nicole called.

When Cindy returned to the table, she looked at the cold soufflé on her plate without enthusiasm.

"Have some spinach salad," Nicole offered.

"What are you—on a spinach kick?" Cindy complained.

"It was on special at the supermarket; besides, it's good for you."

"I thought we were going to have fun while

Mom and Dad were gone," Mollie said. "You sound just like Mother."

Nicole, who normally would have considered the last remark a compliment, couldn't ignore the indignation in her sister's voice. "Somebody has to keep you in line!"

"Who says?" Cindy demanded.

"We're not babies," Mollie added.

"I'm not breaking my back for two people who don't even appreciate my effort," Nicole told them, putting down her fork. "Tomorrow Cindy can cook dinner, and Mollie the day after."

"Fine," her sisters chorused. They finished the meal in gloomy silence. Mollie, who had hoped to talk about her problems at school, felt too out-of-sorts to bring up the subject.

When they finished, Nicole broke the silence to say, "Cindy can clean up the dishes; Mollie, you sweep the floor and take out the garbage."

Cindy rose from her chair and tossed a smart salute toward her older sister. "Heil, Hitler!"

Nicole gave her sister a nasty look and stalked out of the kitchen.

"What's with her, anyway?" Mollie asked as she went to get the broom.

"Delusions of adulthood," Cindy grumbled, eyeing the pots and pans with strong dislike.

When the kitchen was restored to order, Mollie asked, "What are you doing now?"

"Going over to Anna's" was the blithe reply.

"Oh." Mollie, who had briefly hoped for sympathy from Cindy, shrugged. She returned to her room and considered calling Arlene, with whom, until now, she had spent hours on the phone every day. But a happy recounting of the joys of her older group, reunited at Westside, was more than she could bear. Sighing, Mollie opened her history textbook.

Thursday morning was gray and overcast. Even though Mollie knew that the coastal clouds would burn off later in the day and give way to the usual bright sunshine, she felt that the cloudy morning perfectly suited her mood.

She rode to school beside Cindy without talking. Cindy, in high spirits, didn't even notice her sister's lack of enthusiasm.

In algebra class the teacher began by handing back the pretests the class had taken the day before. When Mollie received her paper, she felt her mouth drop open. A sinking feeling in her stomach made her gulp. Half of her problems had been marked wrong.

"Don't fall out of your chair," the boy across the aisle told her.

"What?" Mollie's glance was abstracted.

"You look pretty uptight."

Mollie showed him her red-spattered paper. "Look!"

He shrugged. "Mine's worse. Doesn't matter. She's not going to count it."

Mollie nodded. "I know." But what if I can't learn algebra? she thought.

The teacher rapped on her desk, and the class became quiet. Mollie stared at her desk. She was going to fail algebra; she could see it now. Nobody in her family had ever failed before. Nicole always made the dean's list and Cindy did okay. What would her parents say?

"Mollie Lewis?" The teacher's gaze held her like an amoeba under a microscope.

"Yes?"

"Would you open your book with the rest of us, please?"

As Mollie hurriedly opened her book, her cheeks burned under the stares of her classmates.

No doubt about it; high school was a disaster!

It was a relief when the bell signaled the end of the period. Mollie made a careful note of the homework assignment—no more daydreaming in this class!—and headed thankfully for the door.

She was surprised and pleased to see Nicole waiting in the hall.

"Hi." Mollie grinned, pleased that Nicole had come by to give her a friendly boost.

"I had a student council meeting first hour and didn't get to French," Nicole said. "Would you give this book to Madame Preston for me? I promised her I'd return it today."

"Oh." Mollie's pleasure dimmed abruptly. Nicole only wanted an errand run. "Sure."

"Merci," Nicole said. "I've got to run; don't be late."

"I know that much," Mollie answered, exasperated, but Nicole was already hurrying down the hall.

The French classroom was almost filled with students when Mollie arrived. She went up to the teacher's desk.

"Bonjour, Mollie."

"Uh ... *bonjour,* Madame Preston," Mollie answered. Then—her brief French vocabulary exhausted—she added, "Here's the book Nicole wanted to return. She had a student council meeting this morning."

"Yes, I saw the notice." The teacher nodded. She added a sentence in rapid French.

Mollie, blinking, guessed that it was either a thank-you or a dismissal, or both. She grinned weakly and went to find a seat.

The dark-haired boy waved at her, but Mollie managed to avoid him. She noticed Sarah and her friend, but their glances were not friendly. She sat down in the back of the room by herself.

The first half of the class passed quickly as the teacher led them through a drill in French verbs. Then she introduced a new activity.

"We'll divide into smaller groups so you may practice your vocabulary on one another. Use the words from your first two lessons, and if you need a word you don't know, use the French-English dictionaries in the back of the room.

Oh, great, Mollie thought, watching two boys pass out dictionaries. Which group would she end up in?

Of course, it would be Sarah's.

"If it isn't the French expert," Sarah muttered to her friend as Mollie joined them.

"No." Mollie said horrified. "I'm not ... I never said that. I said I liked French, not that I knew all about it; I'm just a beginner like you," Mollie tried to explain.

"A beginner," Sarah laughed, while Mollie tried to figure out what Sarah's comment meant. Then she added, "Since we're not even human beings, I guess we just don't know how to impress the teacher."

Mollie's patience had its limits. "I didn't say ... she's not that kind of teacher. You certainly like to jump to conclusions, don't you?"

"We're supposed to be speaking French," a thin girl with glasses interrupted, her tone worried as she glanced toward the teacher. The other girls, all wearing militant expressions, hastily opened their books.

"*Bonjour,*" Sarah said. "*Tu est*"—she paused to flip through the French dictionary and then looked up at Mollie—"*un coq.*"

Mollie, who had never been insulted in a foreign language before, looked perplexed.

The blonde stared over her friend's shoulder at the page and giggled. "Cock-a-doodle-do!" she crowed.

"What?" Mollie turned the pages of her dictionary until she located the unfamiliar word. "A rooster? Well, you are, I mean, *tu est un porc!* Oink, oink!"

Mrs. Preston, walking among the different groups and listening to the students' faltering attempts in a new language, glanced toward the group of girls at the back of the room. They all appeared unusually involved in the oral exercise, fluttering pages with great zeal, then pausing to produce a labored sentence. Although she was too far away to distinguish the words, Mrs. Preston smiled at the intensity of their responses.

"Très bon, mes jeune filles," she told them cheerfully as she approached, smiling to herself as they all blushed at her commendation. How nice it was to see such an earnest group of students.

By the time lunchtime came, Mollie felt as if the morning had stretched on for a week. She walked to the cafeteria with lagging steps, then stopped at the side of the room looking for Cindy.

Instead she recognized another face. At the end of a long table nearby Sarah and her friend were seated, already eating and deep in conversation. Mollie grimaced and started to walk away. But it was too late; they had already noticed her.

"If it isn't our friend from French," Sarah said loudly. *"Bonjour,* Madame Expert!"

"I told you—" Mollie began, but Sarah wasn't listening.

Instead she raised her half-filled glass with a flourish.

Mollie had had just about enough. "I'll make a toast now!" she cried, reaching for the glass. Startled, Sarah tightened her grip, and for a moment both girls tugged, then Mollie exerted all her strength, and the glass slipped through the other girl's fingers. But the liquid inside, propelled by the forceful movement, flew out of the glass, sprinkling Mollie and showering someone behind her, who gasped.

"I didn't mean—" Mollie began, turning quickly.

A stout woman, her blue blouse darkened with patches of dampness, glared at the shrinking Mollie. The table of students, who had begun to giggle, quieted abruptly.

"We'll discuss this in the office," the angry teacher said. "Follow me!"

Mollie shuddered and felt her face burning hot. Over the heads of the other freshmen, she saw Cindy—her eyes wide in surprise. There was no time to explain. Glancing desperately at her sister, Mollie followed the stiff, outraged back of the milk-spattered teacher.

Chapter 5

*W*hen Cindy saw Mollie throw a glass of milk onto the most notoriously bad-tempered teacher at Vista High, her eyes widened in shock. For as long as she could remember, Cindy was always the one getting in trouble and Mollie the one who managed to avoid it. As Cindy watched her sister being marched away, her awe gave way to an irrepressible desire to laugh.

Anna finally thumped her on the back. "Stop howling; you sound like a hyena."

"But it's so funny," Cindy protested. "Did you see the look on Mrs. Smith's face?"

"What about the look on Mollie's face?"

"Oh, Mollie will smile sweetly at Mr. Cochran and be out of the office in ten minutes."

"I hope so," Anna murmured. "Look out—here comes Duffy."

"He must have cooled off by now." Cindy wrinkled her nose at the approaching boy.

"I hope you're right."

Cindy apparently was right. Duffy simply stopped at the end of their table and grinned at them. "What are you eating, Lewis? Frogs' legs?"

"Very funny." Cindy grinned. "How's Mary Ann?"

"When she starts talking to me again, I'll let you know." Duffy's grin seemed forced, but he lingered at their table as if he had something else to say.

"Coming to practice this afternoon?" Cindy asked him.

"Didn't you know?" Duffy raised his sandy brows. "Returning team members don't have to come today; it's only for freshmen and new players."

"Great!" Cindy picked up the remains of her lunch. "I can go down to the beach; no one is home to mind if I'm late for dinner. Want to come?"

"Sure, see you there," Duffy agreed.

As Cindy and Anna walked out of the cafeteria, Cindy turned to her friend. "See, I told you he'd get over it."

"I guess," Anna said.

Once, during her next class, Cindy wondered about Mollie's fate, but she had gotten into worse trouble herself before, so she didn't think much about it. She considered waiting and checking up on Mollie after school, but that would spoil her plans to leave early.

Mollie would be all right, Cindy told herself. At the end of the period, catching sight of Nicole in the hall, she ran up to speak to her sister.

"Keep an eye out for Mollie after school," she told Nicole.

"Why?"

"She could be in the doghouse; she threw milk on Mrs. Smith."

"What?" Nicole's exclamation was shrill; heads turned to stare at them both.

"Got to run," Cindy called, already halfway down the hall. "Mollie will explain." She continued toward her locker, unaware of the horrified expression on her older sister's face.

"Detention—the second day of school!" Mollie bit her lip. It was bad enough that she'd been required to stay thirty minutes after school while she wrote a letter of apology to the teacher she had accidentally showered with milk, but to find an outraged Nicole lying in wait for her was worse.

"It was an accident," Mollie replied defensively.

"Throwing milk on a teacher? What kind of an accident is that?" Nicole's voice was sharp with anger.

It was too much. It had been difficult enough trying to explain her unlikely mishap to a skeptical assistant principal, but her own sister should be ready to listen to *her* side. Mollie planted her hands on her hips.

"Will you lay off? I've had enough lectures for one day!"

Nicole's usually gentle eyes sparkled with annoyance. "Home!" she commanded.

Mollie retrieved her bike and rode ahead of her sister, her shoulders hunched in angry despair. Nobody was on her side!

Cindy took advantage of her early exit from school, pedaling home furiously. A quick change, then she lashed her surfboard to the rack on her bike and she was off to the beach.

Blocks away she could smell the salt in the breeze and feel the tang of sea spray against her face. Cindy grinned. This was her favorite place in all the world. She hastily chained her bike to a rack and unloaded the board, stopping only long enough to pull off the shorts and T-shirt that covered her swimsuit and to apply a generous amount of white sunblock to her peeling nose. Then she ran over the hardpacked sand toward the ocean.

The water was cold, and the first shock of it made Cindy catch her breath. Then, laughing in sheer exultation, she dived headfirst beneath the next wave, emerging amid the foam as the wave receded. Climbing onto her board, Cindy lay down and began to pull toward the deeper water, her strokes strong and confident.

Eyeing an approaching wave, she knelt on the board, waiting for the wave to crest. Cindy saw Anna, a tiny figure on the beach, and waved. Anna waved back, then settled decorously onto her towel.

Cindy, shaking her head at anyone who would pass up fun like this to lie on the sand, forgot her friend as the wave surged beneath her. This was living!

Many waves later, Cindy pulled her board up the wet sand and collapsed onto the towel spread out beside her friend. "Did you bring some cola?"

Anna fished in her large beach bag and pulled out two cans. She handed one to Cindy, who pulled back the tab and took a hearty swig. The liquid was slightly warm, but it still felt good to her parched throat.

"Wonder what happened to Duffy," Anna said idly as she applied more suntan oil to her already brown shoulders.

"What?" For the first time Cindy, looking around, noticed something unusual. "Or Lee or Randy," she added. Most of her crowd spent all their free time at the beach, and they all gathered at the same spot. A seed of apprehension threatened her sunny mood, and Cindy sat up straighter. The longer she considered, the more certain her awful suspicion became.

"Anna," she said, her tone ominous, "there are no water polo players on the beach. Except me."

"So?"

"I think I've been had!" Cindy grabbed her beach towel and quickly pulled on her clothes, slipping on the sand in her haste. "Take my surfboard home."

"What?" Anna looked indignant. "You know how heavy that thing is."

"I have to go back to school."

"What for?"

"Practice," Cindy yelled, hurrying up the beach, throwing little spurts of sand behind her as she ran.

It seemed to take much longer than usual to get back to school, detour around the gym, and head for the outdoor pool at the end of the school property.

To Cindy's dismay the pool was well populated with swimmers—not just freshmen—and she could hear Coach Lawford shouting instructions. At the near end, several freshmen practiced their egg-beaters while Coach yelled, "Keep it up!"

Cindy dropped her bike onto the grass and ran into the pool enclosure, slowing suddenly before the coach turned. She was in enough trouble without breaking any more rules. In a very rapid walk, she headed for the pool.

"Well, if it isn't Miss Lewis. Decide to fit us into your busy schedule, did you?"

Cindy felt her cheeks flame. She was never late to practice; this was terrible. "Coach, I was told—I mean, I thought I didn't have to come today."

"Where would you get a harebrained idea like that?" the coach roared.

From the corner of her eye, Cindy could see Duffy, Randy, and several other players pausing at the end of the pool to listen. Duffy grinned widely and Cindy gritted her teeth.

"Dumb, I know," she agreed.

"That's right." Coach Lawford nodded his head. "And since you've missed most of practice, why don't you do a few laps to limber up—like a couple of hundred."

Cindy, who could see the boys in the pool chuckling, wanted to say something, but she just bit her lip. Sometimes, her dad said, you just had to grin and bear it. This sure looked like one of those times.

Managing the best grin she could, Cindy nodded. "Okay."

The boys in the pool looked disappointed at this anticlimax. Cindy got her reward when the coach suddenly noticed the players idling at the water's edge.

"What is this—recess?"

The boys hastened back to their practice as Cindy quickly pulled off her clothes and slipped into the water. After her vigorous surfing, just the thought of all those laps made her whole body ache. With a sigh, she turned toward the far end of the pool, pulling herself smoothly through the water.

She was the last one out of the pool; all of the

other team members had already dressed and departed. But when Cindy climbed out of the water, one player walked toward her.

"Hi, Duffy," Cindy said. She was too tired to harbor any resentment.

"Mad?"

"No, I deserved it, I guess. Hope Mary Ann's not still mad at you."

Duffy shrugged. "It doesn't matter. You were right; she does scream a lot."

They laughed together, and Cindy didn't feel quite so tired. But the ride home brought back all her aches, and her tired muscles protested at each turn of the pedal. It seemed forever until her home came into view. As she pulled her bike into the garage, Cindy was glad she didn't have a lot of homework.

As she walked into the kitchen, she sniffed the air expectantly—no smell of cooking. What was Nicole up to?

As if in answer, her older sister walked through the swinging door. "Where on earth have you been?"

"Practice," Cindy told her.

"Till this hour?"

"I was late; it's a long story. What's for dinner?"

"That's up to you," her sister pointed out in a lofty tone that made Cindy wish she had something handy to toss at her. "It's your turn to cook, remember?"

Cindy groaned. "I forgot."

"I didn't. Hurry up; we're starved."

Nicole left the kitchen, and Cindy dropped her books on the counter and ran one hand through her wet hair. Cindy's culinary skills were virtually limited to brownies. Although Mollie might not mind it, Nicole would surely turn up her nose at brownies for dinner.

She went to the pantry and opened the door, studying the contents and hoping for inspiration. Something soft touched her ankle and Cindy jumped.

Glancing down, she saw Smokey, who rubbed herself against Cindy's bare legs, purring.

"Not now, Smokey, I'm busy," Cindy told the cat as she made a mental inventory. Tomato sauce, yes, and some spaghetti. That was one thing she did know how to make. She took several cans of sauce to the electric can opener, opened the first one, reached for a saucepan, and promptly fell over a large black body, causing tomato sauce to fly across the kitchen.

"For crying out loud, Winston." Cindy, thoroughly exasperated, wet a paper towel and wiped the sauce off the dog's fur while he shoved his damp muzzle into her face. With both cats rubbing against her legs, Cindy tried to clean up the rest of the mess. Finally, she opened the garage door and yelled, "Everybody out!" The dog went at her command; the cats had to be forced. Alone at last, Cindy returned to her cooking.

When she called her sisters to eat, Mollie and Nicole came quickly to the table.

"It's about time," Mollie said. "I'm starved. Where are the napkins?"

"I forgot to put them out; get them yourself." Cindy, who was trying to pour the cooked noodles into a colander and not lose the whole thing down the drain, was too preoccupied to look up. When she brought the filled plates to the table, the other two girls stared suspiciously at the food.

"Why are the noodles all stuck together?" Mollie asked.

"Beats me," Cindy told her. "Use your knife."

"Cindy," Nicole said, "this sauce is like soup. How long did you cook it?"

"About fifteen minutes." Cindy tried to wrap a long piece of spaghetti around her fork.

"It's supposed to simmer for two hours!"

"You said you were hungry," Cindy reminded her. "Eat."

"This stuff is awful. I'm getting a peanut butter sandwich," Mollie complained.

"After all the trouble I went through?" Cindy looked outraged. Nicole grinned, and Cindy realized that this whole conversation had a familiar ring.

"Wait till I tell Mom I was forced to live on peanut butter for two weeks," Mollie said.

"You'd better not!" Cindy glared at the youngest Lewis.

"If you do—" Nicole said at the same time.

"Okay, already," Mollie said. "But can't we have something decent to eat tomorrow?"

"You'll just complain," Cindy told her, still smarting from being on the other side of the cooking apron. "Uh-oh, you're supposed to cook tomorrow."

Even Nicole, who knew it was her idea, looked dubious.

"She doesn't know how to cook anything," Cindy told Nicole over Mollie's head.

"That's not true," Mollie tried to interrupt.

"We'll probably have peanut butter sandwiches and fudge."

"I guess it's time she learned, then," Nicole suggested.

"Not if *we* have to eat it," Cindy argued.

Mollie, insulted by her sisters' lack of confidence in her, said, "Whatever I fix couldn't be any worse than this mess!" She picked up her fork, and a large gob of spaghetti came with it.

"Listen." Cindy's tone was indignant. "At least I tried."

"Stop it, both of you!"

"Don't be so darned bossy!" Cindy snapped.

"Somebody has to be in charge!" Nicole's face turned red.

"Who says?"

"If you're going to be late every night—"

"I won't be late every night; if I hadn't missed half of practice—" Too late she remembered that she hadn't meant to share that story.

But Nicole pounced. "What were you doing missing practice? Isn't it bad enough, Mollie getting detention the second day of high school—"

"Oh, did you?" Cindy asked with real interest.
Mollie made a face.

"And now you seem to need supervision as
well!" Nicole finished.

"Give me a break, Nicole," Cindy protested. "I
do not. Duffy told me I didn't have to go, because
... well, that's a long story, too."

"And you believed him? Talk about dumb."

"Shut up!" Cindy yelled. "Being two years older
doesn't make you perfect! And it certainly doesn't
give you the right to boss me around."

Nicole flushed in anger. "Do you think I *like*
trying to keep you two birdbrains in line? *Mon
Dieu!*"

"Then stop!"

"Fine, I will!"

The girls paused. Mollie stared at them both
uncertainly.

"Meaning?" the youngest Lewis asked.

"Meaning you two can take care of yourselves.
If you don't have a decent dinner or any clean
clothes to wear, too bad! You don't want my help,
you're not going to get it!" Nicole pushed her
chair back from the table and stood up. "From
now on it's every woman for herself!"

"Great!" the other two girls agreed.

Nicole stalked toward the door, pausing to ask
in disgust, "What *is* this sticky stuff on the floor?"

Cindy shut her eyes.

Chapter 6

*M*ollie awoke Friday morning feeling irritable, although she couldn't remember why until she clicked off her buzzing alarm and sat up in bed to stretch. Another day in high school—what a depressing thought.

She considered crawling back under the covers, but Nicole would just come and yell at her. Besides, what would Mom say if she found out that Mollie had skipped school? Mollie swallowed experimentally—no sign of a sore throat. No stuffy nose, no fever.

Face it—she was doomed to another day with classmates who disliked her and didn't care about showing it. Talking to Arlene last night had only made her feel worse. Westside High sounded terrific, and she couldn't help feeling jealous of her friends, who were having such an easy time. Sighing, Molly climbed out of bed.

Going into the bathroom to wash her face, she encountered a sleepy-eyed Cindy, pulling a comb through her hair.

"Move over," Mollie said.

Cindy grunted and allowed her sister room before the mirror.

Going back to her bedroom, Mollie opened her closet door and tried to decide what to wear. Not that it really mattered, she told herself. Still, she couldn't help hoping that today someone might notice her.

Her new plaid skirt—but where was the blouse that went with it?

"It's in the clothes hamper," Mollie answered herself.

Was there time to wash and dry it before school? Maybe. Mollie ran to the bathroom and rummaged through the dirty clothes until she found her blouse, then ran down the stairs two at a time.

Nicole wasn't in the kitchen, and there was no sign of breakfast. Mollie was puzzled until she remembered their agreement. "Every woman for herself." Okay. She'd eat a bowl of cereal, but first the blouse.

In the laundry room Mollie raised the lid of the washing machine and dropped the blouse inside. Reaching for the box of detergent, she glanced uncertainly over the instructions on the back.

"I wonder how much this will take," she said aloud. Then, aware of the time, she shrugged and tipped the box over the open washer.

"That should be enough," she told Smokey, who jumped lightly onto the top of the washing machine and poked an inquisitive nose into the box of detergent, then sneezed loudly.

"Silly," Mollie laughed. She pulled the knob and, as water poured into the machine, returned to the kitchen to locate the cereal.

"Better hurry, Mollie." Nicole came into the kitchen, already dressed and ready for school. "Where's Cindy?"

"I don't know. Want some cereal?"

"I made myself an omelet an hour ago." Nicole's tone was smug. Mollie made a face at her.

Nicole, ignoring the childish insult, disappeared through the swinging door.

Mollie rinsed out her bowl and glass and put them into the dishwasher, then went to check on her blouse. But when she opened the laundry room door, she couldn't believe her eyes. She gasped in horror as she watched suds pour out of the washer, spilling over the smooth enamel top and drenching the tile floor.

"Oh, no!" Mollie moaned, and stood for a moment, uncertain what to do.

Her first impulse was to call Nicole for help. Then she remembered their new agreement and Mollie's resolve hardened. She was certainly not going to admit to being unable to cope on her own. It was bad enough being the baby of the family without such an obvious display of incompetence.

Grabbing a large sponge from the laundry tub, she tried wiping off the side of the washer, but this attempt was useless, as sudsy water continued to overflow. It finally occurred to Mollie to switch off the machine. Her blouse would have to wait for another day. But what about the floor?

The mop, of course. Mollie ran for the sponge mop and tried to soak up the water.

"Mollie, where are you? I'm leaving," Cindy called from the kitchen.

"Go ahead," Mollie answered quickly. She didn't want anyone to see this mess. "I'll leave in a few minutes."

"Don't be late; you'll get in trouble again," her sister warned.

"Right." Molly mopped for dear life.

Cindy, pedaling rapidly toward the school, wondered if she should have waited for Mollie. But she wasn't a baby, and Cindy didn't want to be late.

Anna and Carey were waiting at her locker, and the morning passed quickly until it was time for Spanish. Then, as Cindy pulled her textbook out of the bottom of her locker, Anna peered anxiously over her shoulder.

"You do have your workbook, don't you?"

"Sure." Cindy continued to dig into the chaotic contents of their locker. "It's got to be here someplace."

"You know how mad Mrs. Lopez got yesterday

when half the class forgot their workbooks. She promised extra assignments to anyone who forgets today."

Cindy continued to claw through the disorganized stack of books and papers. "Oh, no!"

"What?"

"I left it on my desk at home. What am I going to do?"

"You're going to get stuck with all that extra work," Anna told her.

"Wait a minute. I've got an idea. Go on to class; I'll be there in a minute."

Cindy took off down the hall at a run, almost colliding with a bunch of boys from the water polo team. One of them called out, "Late for practice, Cindy?"

But Cindy was intent on only one thing—catching Nicole, who had the next period free to work on the yearbook or take an early lunch. Fortunately, she glimpsed her sister ahead.

"Nicole!"

"What's the matter?" Nicole looked startled as Cindy galloped up and grabbed her arm.

"I've got Spanish next, and I left my workbook at home. Will you run home and get it for me? It's on my desk."

Nicole appeared unmoved by this emergency. "Why should I do that? I thought you didn't want my help."

Cindy's hopeful expression altered quickly at

this unexpected refusal. "Forget it!" She left as quickly as she'd come.

"What's between you two?" the short, blond girl beside Nicole commented.

"If you'd heard those two brats last night," Nicole complained, "you'd understand. They can't have it both ways. They don't want my advice, but they want me to pull them out of trouble. Is that fair?"

"I guess not," Bitsy agreed. "Coming into the cafeteria?"

Nicole glanced at her watch. "I told Angela I'd wait for her."

"Again?" Bitsy asked sarcastically. "You're spending all your time with Angela; your *old friends* are beginning to forget what you look like."

"Stay and eat with us, then," Nicole urged.

But Bitsy shook her head, her blond curls swinging in defiance. "No way. I know exactly what will happen. Angela will start telling us how second-rate California is compared to New York, and how crude the people are—including yours truly. She gives me indigestion."

"But ..." Nicole began, when the two girls saw Angela at the end of the hall, "she's so interesting."

"So's a shark, but I don't want to share a meal with one," Bitsy retorted. "See you later."

"Okay," Nicole said, feeling guilty because she recognized the truth in Bitsy's words. Angela did sometimes make derogatory comments, but Nicole told herself that Angela was simply homesick and hadn't adjusted yet to the move. In time she would see that living on the West Coast did have some advantages, and curb her acidic wit. At least, Nicole certainly hoped so, before she lost all of her old friends.

"Hi," she said now. "Ready to eat?"

"In that place? No, thanks. I don't really have an appetite for that garbage." Angela arched her finely plucked brows.

"Well . . ." Nicole, who tended to look on the positive side, sounded dubious. "The salad bar's pretty good; why don't you try that?"

"Nicole," Angela said, "I exhausted the possibilities of that place the first day of school. Which reminds me, I have a recipe for Cassoulet de Mer you've got to try."

"Terrific," Nicole said. Angela's love of French cooking was turning out to be one of their strongest bonds. Angela could be fascinating to talk to when she turned to the interests that both girls shared. And she was so cultured—unlike many of Nicole's friends, who were too preoccupied with boys to talk about much else. As for the rest, it was true Angela could be too critical, but she didn't seem to have made any friends besides Nicole. And Nicole, who had a tendency to mother, could hardly abandon a homesick and probably— despite her brave pretense—unhappy girl.

After school Mark drove Nicole home. When she walked into the kitchen, she found the remains of yet another peanut butter sandwich and an almost empty glass of milk on the breakfast table. Shaking her head—Mollie and her peanut butter; had the kids tasted a vegetable or fruit this week?—Nicole started to call her little sister to clean up her mess, then hesitated. She'd tell her later; Nicole was too tired to jump into a new argument.

And she was hungry herself. It didn't seem worth the trouble to cook a proper dinner just for herself—nor did it seem exactly fair to her sisters. But they'd asked for it, Nicole reminded herself.

Still ... both cats were winding themselves about her ankles, and Nicole broke her train of thought to stoop and pet them.

But Smoked yowled once, unappeased. Nicole raised her brows.

"Are you hungry? I bet no one remembered to feed you—those brats!"

She went to the cupboard and got down the cat food, filled their dishes with food and clean water, and went to check on Winston.

The big black dog was lying on his bed at the end of the garage. He raised his head hopefully when she walked out of the kitchen.

"Hungry, Winston?"

A deep woof was her answer, and the dog jumped up in his awkward enthusiasm, almost pushing her down.

"Winston, down!"

He followed her eagerly into the kitchen, and she could barely get the dog food into his dish before he gobbled up the bowlful.

"I bet you weren't fed last night either, poor baby." Nicole rubbed Winston's big shaggy head and his tail wagged briskly, sounding a staccato beat against the cabinet.

Now that the pets had been cared for, Nicole washed her hands and made herself a salad. When she finished, she put her dishes into the dishwasher and went into the laundry room to fold some towels. The condition of the room left her speechless; pools of water stood on the tile floor.

"Mollie!" Nicole shrieked.

"What is it?" Alarmed by the consternation in her sister's voice, Mollie came running.

"Did you do this?"

Mollie bit her lip. "I was trying to wash my blouse. The machine overflowed."

"How much detergent did you put in?"

"I'm not sure."

Nicole groaned. "Why didn't you clean it up?"

"I thought I did. I didn't want to be late for school."

"You mean this happened this morning?" Nicole's rage seemed to redouble. "All this water might ruin the floor. Get the rest of this water up, right now!"

"Okay, already." Mollie's own sense of guilt

simply increased her irritability. Grumbling, she went for the mop.

Nicole, shaking her head, went upstairs.

When Cindy got home after practice, she was still annoyed with Nicole. It wouldn't have been any trouble for her to have collected the workbook. Nicole could really be a pain. Now Cindy was stuck with two extra assignments, and she'd have no time left for telephone calls to her friends or her favorite television show.

Cindy, remembering that no one was scheduled to cook dinner, had stopped at Taco Rico on her way home from school and used the last of her allowance to buy a sack of tacos and burritos. After she parked her bike in the garage, Winston came to greet her with a friendly woof, sniffing at the paper bag in her hand.

"No, Winston, that's my dinner. Are you hungry?"

The dog still showed interest in the bag, with its savory meat aroma. Cindy shook her head.

"Bet no one remembered to feed you. Come on, big boy."

She set her dinner safely out of reach on the counter and opened a can of dog food, watching Winston lick his bowl clean.

"You were hungry, all right. Nicole could have thought to feed you." Cindy checked the cat's dishes, added a little food though they were half-full, and replaced them on the shelf above Winston's head to keep the greedy canine from using their dinners as snacks.

"I've got to get to work, worse luck. See you later, boy." Cindy poured herself some soda, searched the refrigerator for anything else worth eating, and finally picked up her bag of food and her books and headed for her room.

On the stairs she passed Nicole and considered making a cool remark about her neglecting the animals; but she decided she was still too miffed to speak, so the sisters passed each other in haughty silence.

Nicole found Mollie in the family room, watching a video. "Did you get up all the water? What about the dishes you left in the kitchen?"

Mollie sighed. "Don't you ever let up?"

"And don't forget your homework."

Mollie stamped off to the kitchen and cleared away her dishes. Winston came forward and sniffed at the remains of her sandwich.

"Oh, Winston, are you hungry, baby?" Mollie cooed. "Just a minute."

She opened a can of dog food and dumped it into his dish. He ate it more slowly than usual, she thought. "Not sick, are you, Winnie?"

The big Newfoundland wagged his heavy tail, and she patted his head. "*You* care about me, don't you, Winnie?"

Upstairs, Cindy chewed on the end of her pencil as she tried to concentrate on her Spanish, but she couldn't stop thinking that it was all Nicole's fault for not helping her out. As if her thought had conjured up her older sister, Nicole suddenly put her head inside the doorway of the bedroom.

"Don't forget I'm going tomorrow to that art exhibit."

"Well, don't look at me," Cindy responded quickly. "I've got plans, too."

"Cindy, you live at that beach. I've waited all summer for this exhibit, and it's only there for one more week."

"What's so great about a bunch of paintings, anyhow?" Cindy grumbled, adding hastily as Nicole seemed about to argue the point, "Never mind, I don't want to know. They're French, I'm sure. Anyway, Mollie's old enough to stay by herself. Stop being such a mother hen."

"I said I'm not giving any more advice, and I'm not." Nicole's answer was heated. "Do what you want, and see if I care!"

"That's fine with me, Miss Priss." Cindy's voice rose, too. "Lay off, will you? You didn't even remember to feed the dog."

"I did, too. I fed him right after school."

"Oh." Cindy's ire faded. "I fed him, too. He looked hungry."

"Oh, no," Nicole said. "You know what a pig Winston is. I hope—"

But Nicole wasn't able to finish, because a sudden shriek from downstairs made them both jump, then run to the stairs.

"Nicole, Cindy," Molly wailed. "Winston's sick!"

"Get him outside, quick," Nicole answered as she ran down the stairs, followed closely by her sister.

"Too late," Mollie groaned. "He's in the living room." Looking distinctly green, she ran for the bathroom.

Nicole and Cindy looked at each other.

"Get the paper towels; I'll find the carpet cleaner," Nicole said.

"It's not my fault!" Cindy, her nose wrinkled, looked less than enthusiastic.

"You fed him, too."

"Well, how was I to know—"

"If we don't get this up right now, it'll make a permanent stain, and I'm not taking all the blame for this."

Cindy made a face and went for the paper towels. When she joined Nicole in the living room, she grumbled, "Why isn't Mollie helping?"

"Mollie!" Nicole called. "Get in here and help us."

"I can't," came the muffled reply.

"Yes, you can, and you better get in here right now!" Nicole yelled.

In a moment Mollie came slowly down the staircase. Nicole tossed her youngest sister a sponge.

"Get a pail of warm water," she commanded. "Cindy, go get the stain remover; I don't think this cleaner is strong enough to do the job."

Mollie, holding the sponge at arm's length as if it were going to bite her, shuddered while she rubbed her portion of the carpet gingerly, holding her nose. "I can't do this, Nicole. I'm going to be sick."

"No, you're not. Stop being such a baby!"

"I'm not a baby," Mollie wailed. "You're mean."

"So take me out of your will." Nicole sounded unimpressed. "Meanwhile, scrub harder."

Cindy returned with a bottle of liquid and immediately poured a good part of the bottle onto the soiled carpet.

"What do you think you're doing?" Nicole shrieked.

"I'm doing what you *told* me to," Cindy bellowed.

"Not the whole bottle, you ninny. You'll take all the color out of the carpet."

"I was just trying to help." Cindy glared back at her sister.

"If you'd listen to instructions—"

"Some instructions! You didn't say how much; you blew it, kid."

"It's not my—" Nicole began, then turned her head. "Mollie, exactly where do you think you're going?"

"To the bathroom." Mollie, caught in the act of slipping out of the room, looked guilty.

"Get back here! If we don't get this stain up—"

"I can't!"

Even Cindy threw Mollie a disgusted look. "What a sissy!"

"I am not!" Mollie stamped her foot.

A sudden shrill ring made them all pause. "I'll

get it," Mollie yelled, and made good her escape from the room.

Nicole sighed and pushed back a lock of brown hair with her elbow. "If this leaves a stain, Mother will kill us."

"Nicole," Mollie called from the kitchen. "It's Mark. He's on his way over."

"Oh, no," Nicole groaned.

Chapter 7

*N*icole *dropped her sponge and hurried to the* phone.

"Like me to come over and bring a pizza?" Mark asked.

Nicole swallowed hard. "I don't think so, Mark. I'm not really in the mood to eat right now."

"Want to watch a movie? I could rent a tape for the VCR."

Nicole, thinking of the condition of the living room, sighed. She'd die if Mark saw the house right now. "Mark, I don't feel like doing anything tonight; do you mind? And we wanted to get an early start tomorrow, anyhow."

"That's okay."

"Mad?" Nicole's tone was anxious.

"Nope. I'll just eat the whole pizza myself." Mark laughed.

"Have fun," she told him. "I'll see you tomorrow at nine."

Going back to the living room, where Cindy, on her hands and knees, continued to scrub the carpet, Nicole murmured, "I never thought I'd turn down a date with Mark for this!"

But the evening wasn't over yet. When Nicole emerged from the shower, she found Mollie waiting for her outside the bathroom, a plaintive look on her face.

"What's the matter?"

"I've got a terrible stomachache."

Nicole looked at her sister's white face and visualized a huge stack of peanut butter sandwiches. "That's not surprising. Take a spoonful of that pink stuff Mother gives you, and drink a glass of fruit juice before you go to bed. A *big* glass."

What a day, Nicole thought as she finally escaped to the peaceful haven of her room. Pulling back her sheets, she climbed into bed and laid her cheek against the delicate floral pattern with a sigh of relief. Mothering wasn't as easy as it appeared.

Fortunately, Mollie awoke Saturday morning feeling much better and—determined not to incur any lectures on nutrition—decided to cook herself a proper breakfast. She put on a robe and shuffled down to the kitchen—plugging her nose as she passed the living room—rather pleased with herself for having so much initiative.

While she was pouring herself another glass of juice, she heard a noise in the garage. She froze for a moment, then recognized Winston's familiar snuffling and went to poke her head through the back door.

Cindy, already back from her usual Saturday-morning jog, was sorting through a shelf full of sports equipment.

"What're you doing?"

"Looking for something."

"I can see that!" Mollie, who hated being patronized, waited until Cindy pulled a life jacket from the shelf, and watched her sister rub off the dust.

"Since when do you need a life jacket on the beach? What's it for?"

"Two points for being observant, Sherlock!"

"Come on, Cindy, what's up?"

Cindy glanced toward the open door and lowered her voice. "Don't be so nosy."

Mollie, correctly interpreting this remark, lowered her voice also. "Come on, Cindy, I won't tell."

"Duffy's family has a new sailboat, and we're taking it out for the first time today."

Mollie's eyes widened. "But you've never been on a sailboat!"

"So? There has to be a first time for everybody," Cindy said.

"Does Duffy know how to sail?"

"Sure, he's been out with his uncle once or twice."

Mollie frowned. She had an idea that her parents might not be too thrilled with Cindy's plan. "Do you think you should?"

"You bet," Cindy said. "And if you tell Nicole where I'm going, I'll break your neck!"

"I won't," Mollie promised, then added, "but be careful, Cindy."

"That's why I'm taking the life jacket. Catch you later." Cindy strapped the jacket to her bike rack and mounted. "I may be late."

"Okay." Mollie remembered something. "Cindy?"

"Yes?" Cindy paused as she adjusted the headphones on her portable stereo.

"How do you make scrambled eggs?"

"Put some butter in the pan, then beat up the eggs before you put them in," Cindy replied patiently before pushing off.

Mollie returned to the kitchen, impatiently pushing Winston out of her way. As she went to the refrigerator and took out a stick of butter, milk, eggs, and a package of bacon, the dog followed her hopefully step by step.

"Don't try to tell me you're hungry, you faker," Mollie scolded as he tried to put a broad muzzle into the carton of eggs. "Out!"

Reluctantly the dog padded back to the garage, and Mollie returned to her cooking. How much butter? She put the skillet on the stove, turned on the gas burner, and considered.

It didn't look very big. She dropped the stick into the skillet, where it began at once to melt, then turned her attention to the bacon. She had to consult the microwave cookbook to see how long to cook the strips, then find a glass pan safe to use in the microwave oven. Feeling quite smug that she had remembered not to use a metal pan, Mollie lined the glass dish with bacon strips and covered them with a paper towel. Now . . .

A sudden smell of scorched butter made her turn, and she saw that the melted butter in her skillet was sizzling. She hadn't even broken the eggs yet. She hurried to the sink and took two eggs from the carton and broke them into a bowl, taking a minute to fish out a bit of shell. Going for the milk to add to the eggs—she'd never realized making breakfast was so much work—Mollie could hear the liquefied butter popping in the skillet. Quickly she added milk to her eggs, as her mother did, then decided to add one more egg. She was really hungry. But the slick shell seemed to glide through her fingers, and it landed with a splat on the tile floor.

"Shoot," Mollie exclaimed, turning back to the sink for paper towels.

A crackling sound made her pause, her hands full of toweling.

She glanced toward the stove and froze in horror. The skillet was alight with flames, which were leaping and stretching perilously close to the overhead cabinets.

"Oh, no!" Mollie gasped. She ran to the door and cried, "Nicole!"

There was no answer. Looking back at once at the flaming skillet—how had it happened?—Mollie ran for the stairs.

Nicole's bedroom was empty. Running to the bathroom, Mollie pounded on the locked door.

"Nicole, help!"

But the sound of rushing water and classical music drowned out her cry. Inside the shower, with the radio on, Nicole would never hear her.

Mollie ran back downstairs, almost stumbling over her own feet. Now what?

The telephone! Thank goodness her parents kept emergency numbers taped to the side. Mollie dialed quickly, and when the connection was made, found that she was gasping with shock. She fought to control her voice.

"I've set the kitchen on fire! Come quick!" She managed to stutter her address.

The voice at the other end was lost in a sudden, high-pitched keening that made Mollie drop the phone. Now what? The smoke detector in the hall had gone off, and the ungodly noise simply increased Mollie's terror.

But the shrill whine of the emergency device had an unexpected benefit. Mollie felt rather than heard hurried footsteps on the staircase, and then Nicole, dripping wet, wrapped only in a towel, ran into the kitchen.

"Mollie!" Nicole yelled. "What happened?"

Mollie, beyond coherent speech, could only point to the blazing skillet, while Nicole ran to the pantry and pulled out a small box.

As Mollie watched, frozen in shock and fear, her older sister ran back to the stove and dashed the contents of the box—white powdery stuff—over the fire. The flames flickered, not quite out, although no longer leaping hopefully toward the cabinets above.

But this enabled Nicole to reach to the back of the stove and turn off the burner.

"What is it?" Mollie yelled, her voice shaking.

"Baking soda. Where's the cover?"

Mollie didn't answer. Nicole rummaged through the bottom cupboard until she found the skillet lid. After she slipped the close-fitting lid over the skillet, the last of the flames disappeared beneath the metal cover.

"Are you all right?" Nicole asked, her tone turning to one of annoyance now that the crisis had passed. "How did you manage this one, Mollie?"

Mollie, who was shaking all over, looked crestfallen. "I didn't mean to, Nicole."

"Oh, I know. It's okay, Mollie." Nicole hugged her sister briefly, while surveying the damage to the stove. "What a mess. Next time, don't leave a skillet on the burner like that."

Mollie, grateful to be spared the justified wrath she had dreaded, hugged her sister back, and saw Nicole wince.

"Are you hurt?"

"Just my arm; I think I burned it—" Nicole began before her words were drowned out by the sound of an approaching siren. "What's that?"

"Oh." Mollie remembered her phone call. "Nicole, I—"

But her sister wasn't listening. The insistence of the rapidly approaching siren had drawn her to the window. Mollie followed, and they both saw the fire engine pull up to the curb. Several men jumped off and ran for the house.

"Mollie—" Nicole began, but her sister hurried to open the front door.

"My sister's hurt!" she cried to the young man in the uniform.

He ran quickly into the kitchen, looking around as he sniffed the smoky air.

"It's all right. It was only a grease fire. We put it out," Nicole explained.

"Are you injured?"

"I just burned my arm a little." And Nicole, looking at the young man, remembered that she was wearing nothing but a large bath towel, although not large enough. She thought waves of crimson bathed her cheeks and throat and extended . . . she didn't care to think how far.

"Let me get something on," she stammered.

"Let me see your arm," the young fireman said at the same moment, then grinned at the appeal on her face. "Okay. But I want to see your burns."

Later, when Nicole had hastily pulled on some clothes, and explanations had been given, the

young man examined her reddened skin and announced that her burn, though sore, was super-
ficial.

"Good thing you were wet," he told Nicole,
grinning, and she blushed again.

Meanwhile, several of their neighbors had come
out to see what the fuss was about. After the fire
truck and its crew had departed and the neighbors were reassured as to the girls' safety, Nicole
and Mollie came back into the house and collapsed onto the living room sofa.

"All I meant to do was cook some breakfast,
Nicole," Mollie told her sister. "You said I wasn't
eating properly. I feel terrible that you got burned."

"I'm okay, Mollie," Nicole said. "But someone
has got to give you some cooking lessons. Haven't
you paid any attention to Mother?"

Mollie looked woeful, and Nicole changed the
subject quickly. "Listen, I've got to rush. I'll be
gone most of the day, but tomorrow I'll cook a
real dinner—something you like, okay? I don't
want you dying of an overdose of peanut butter."

Mollie giggled and Nicole felt better. Then the
sound of the doorbell made her jump up.

"That's Mark, and I'm not ready." She ran for
the stairs. "Tell him I'll be down in a few minutes."

Mollie, always happy to talk to Mark, who was
good-natured and laughed at her jokes, went to
let him in. Did she have a story to tell him today!

When Mollie opened the door, Mark's expression was anxious. "Sorry I'm late; I overslept. Is Nicole mad?"

"She's not even ready," Mollie reassured him. "Come in; we've had lots of excitement this morning."

Mollie, who could always tell a dramatic story, had an appreciative audience, and by the time Nicole came downstairs, Mark looked at her with concern.

"Are you all right? Do you think you should go?"

"I'm fine," Nicole reassured him. "Honest. I wouldn't miss this for anything."

"If you're sure."

Touched by his concern, Nicole gave him a light kiss. "You're a doll to worry, but I'm fine. The shock was the worst part."

"I was so scared," Mollie admitted, glad to hear that her sister had found the incident upsetting, too. "I thought I'd burned the whole house down."

"It could have been a disaster," Nicole agreed. "But it wasn't. Mark, I'm ready. Listen, Mollie, don't even go near the stove while I'm gone!"

"I won't, I promise," Mollie told her sister. "I'll eat some cereal. And for lunch I'll make a—"

"Don't say it," Nicole begged. "Eat a piece of fruit, too, please."

They were almost out of the door when the shrill sound of the telephone made Nicole start.

"If that's for me," she told Mollie, "I'm not here."

"No more delays," she promised Mark as he held open the car door. "L.A.—here we come!"

But before Mark could shut his door, Mollie was on the doorstep shrieking, "Nicole, wait!"

"Now what?" Nicole whirled around. But her sister's next sentence made her freeze in horror.

"It's Duffy. Cindy's in the emergency room!"

Chapter 8

$\mathcal{N}$icole jumped out of Mark's car and ran toward the house. "What?"

"Duffy says come quick. Cindy's in the emergency room at the hospital."

"What happened?" Nicole imagined all sorts of terrible things before she took a deep breath to steady herself.

"He didn't tell me. He sounded so excited, and I got so frightened. What do we do?" Mollie's eyes were wide as she waited for guidance from her sister.

"We have to get to the hospital. Better take the station wagon." Nicole found it hard to think clearly.

Behind her, Mark spoke firmly. "Get in my car; I'll drive."

"But—"

"We're wasting time. You can't drive like this. We'll *all* end up in the hospital."

She followed him toward the car, and Mollie ran after them. They all piled into the car, and Mark backed out of the driveway.

"You're sure Duffy didn't say what happened?"

"I told you, Nicole."

"It's probably nothing serious." Mark tried to soothe her, but Nicole kept seeing terrible visions: Cindy crushed beneath a speeding car, Cindy bleeding, Cindy with broken bones—her imagination supplied one dreadful picture after another. She was in charge and she didn't even know where Cindy had gone!

"How will I ever tell Mom and Dad?" Nicole moaned to herself, thinking, It's my fault! Just what it was that she should have done, she wasn't sure, but she felt guilty nonetheless.

In the back seat, Mollie, watching Mark steer carefully and Nicole grip her hands tightly in her lap, struggled with her own guilt. She had known what Cindy was up to, and she hadn't told Nicole, who probably would have forbidden the whole trip.

"It's all my fault," she blurted out just as the hospital came into view. "I should have told you, Nicole."

"Told me what?" Nicole peered at her sister over the seat.

Mollie sobbed. "She went out with Duffy in his new sailboat."

"Oh, terrific." Nicole put her hands to her face. "She's drowned herself!"

"Don't jump to conclusions," Mark warned. "Cindy's an excellent swimmer."

"She took a life jacket," Mollie added brightly.

Some of the strain on Nicole's face eased. "Let us out here while you park the car," she begged Mark. He slowed the vehicle to allow the girls to jump out at the side entrance to the hospital.

Nicole ran through the double doors, followed by her younger sister, and up to the white-clad nurse behind the counter.

"Where's my sister—Cindy Lewis? We were told she'd been admitted."

With maddening deliberation, the woman moved a sheet of paper and glanced down her list of patients. "Yes." She nodded. "She's being examined in the emergency room."

"Is she all right?" Mollie asked.

But Nicole, too impatient to wait for an answer that she dreaded, ran toward the door marked "Patients only."

"Just a minute; you can't go in there," the nurse called, but Nicole ignored her.

Mollie, wide-eyed, hurried after while the nurse made clucking noises and shook her head.

Nicole searched through the row of patients who lay on examining tables, partially hidden by white curtains. An elderly lady, a boy with a bloody knee, then—Cindy!

Cindy lay very still on the long table, her face

pale beneath her tan; her eyes were closed. Nicole's heart jumped to her throat.

"Is she all right?" Nicole begged the doctor who bent over her sister.

"Just a mild concussion," the doctor told her. "She's a lucky girl. The X ray revealed no fractures, but I want her observed closely for forty-eight hours and kept very quiet. If she should begin vomiting or seeing double, you bring her straight back, understand?"

"Yes." Nicole nodded. She came closer to Cindy, touching her sister's arm gently.

"How do you feel?"

"Terrible." Cindy's words were slow and a little slurred. "I think we jibbed when we should have jabbed."

"Sailing a boat is harder than we thought," someone said. For the first time Nicole noticed Duffy, standing quietly next to the wall.

"Of course it is," Nicole snapped.

But the boy's freckled face reflected his recent fright, and when he said, "I thought I'd killed her!" Nicole contained her anger.

"How could you go off like that without telling me what you were doing?" she said, turning to Cindy. Now that she knew Cindy's injury wasn't serious, she felt a strong desire to strangle her.

Cindy, hearing the angry exasperation in her sister's voice, shut her eyes again, murmuring, "My head hurts."

Nicole, left with no one to vent her anger upon, simply shook her head.

But before the hospital released Cindy, there were forms to be filled out, and Nicole had a marvelous argument with the nurse at the front desk, who wanted a parent's signature. The woman finally gave up, and Nicole felt much better.

Supported by Mark and Duffy, Cindy managed to walk to the car. Seeing how shaky her sister was revived all Nicole's anxieties.

Only when Cindy was home in bed did Nicole begin to relax. She left Mollie upstairs to listen for any calls from Cindy, and went back to the family room. Duffy had already left, but Mark was sitting on the sofa. He jumped up when Nicole came into the room.

"How is she?"

"Sleepy."

"She'll be fine, Nicole."

Nicole nodded, coming closer to lean against his shoulder. "Thanks, Mark. You were great."

He hugged her gently. "I guess your weekend is shot."

Nicole, remembering for the first time her long-awaited trip to the art museum, felt a pang of disappointment and tried to tell herself that it didn't matter.

No matter how hard Nicole tried to concentrate on how thankful she was that Cindy wasn't more seriously injured, it did matter. Those paintings were traveling through the country on special loan from several European museums. It might be years, if ever, before she had a chance to see them again.

"*C'est la vie,*" she said slowly. "I'd better clean up Mollie's mess in the kitchen."

"I know you were really looking forward to it," Mark told her, then added, "And you're going to see those paintings."

"How can we?"

Mark grinned at the return of some of her usual sparkle as Nicole waited hopefully for his answer.

"I've got a test on Monday, but let's go on Tuesday. If you don't mind cutting school."

Nicole, who had never even cut a class—let alone a whole day—laughed. "It's worth the risk," she told him. "Mark, you're terrific!"

With Tuesday to look forward to, the weekend passed quickly for Nicole. Cindy made a rapid recovery and moaned about being kept indoors for the rest of the weekend, when the sun shone brightly.

"Everyone's at the beach," she complained Sunday afternoon. "I could lie on a towel and at least talk to my friends. I won't go surfing. Come on, Nicole."

"No way," Nicole told her firmly.

Cindy made a face, but she stayed on the couch, watching old movies on TV and playing with the cats.

Mollie, who was being extra good—and glad

not to think about school—brought her sister endless glasses of juice and generally hung over her until Cindy finally threw a pillow at her.

"Go away; you're driving me nuts!"

"I just wanted to help." Mollie looked hurt.

"I know," Cindy sighed. "Being so still gets on my nerves. If you want to do something, how about a game of rummy?"

"Sure." Mollie brightened at once and went to find a deck of cards. With only occasional arguments, they played for mythical stakes until Cindy was in debt several million bananas.

"That's it," Cindy announced, throwing her cards across the coffee table. "I can't take any more. You'll own my surfboard if we play any longer. What's for dinner, Nicole? Do we get some real food today?"

Nicole, watching the cats pounce on the cards, nodded. "Cinders is eating the Queen of Spades," she told them. Mollie ran to retrieve the cards.

"Dinner's almost ready: pot roast, new potatoes, almond green beans, and fruit salad," she announced triumphantly.

"Yum," Mollie exclaimed, and Cindy's expression of discontent lightened.

On Monday morning Mollie again felt the now familiar depression, but during the weekend she had read an article in *Seventeen* about positive thinking, so she put on an extra dollop of eye makeup and set off for school defiantly.

Cindy had an interesting story to tell at school, or at least—since Duffy had already told his version of their fiasco—she could count on lots of interested listeners for her version of the affair.

"If Duffy would learn which is port and which is starboard, it would help," she told her friends at lunch, amid a chorus of giggles, which made Duffy turn red.

"Hey, I'm not that bad," he protested.

"Listen to the guy talk," Cindy teased. "How many more crew members do you plan to knock senseless?"

Duffy looked perplexed, and Cindy, who was already looking forward to the next opportunity to try sailing, grinned. "Next time I'll wear a helmet," she told him. The kids around them laughed.

On Tuesday Nicole was up early. Although she hadn't slept well—excitement and nervousness about cutting school had made her restless—she didn't feel a bit tired, and she hummed as she put on her favorite outfit, a slim periwinkle-blue skirt with a dusty rose sweater and matching shoes. She considered putting her hair in a bun but opted instead for a French braid. Downstairs, she made herself a light breakfast and sat at the breakfast table to wait for Mark.

For the first time in several days, Mollie was unable to slip out of the house without passing her sister's inspection.

"Where are you going dressed like that?" Nicole exclaimed when she saw Mollie.

"To school, of course." Mollie looked surprised.

"You look like a little girl playing dress-up, and you've put on way too much makeup," her older sister told her sternly.

Molly grimaced. "It's not too much."

"And that sweater's too tight and you know it. What would Mom say if she saw you?"

Mollie preferred not to consider the question. "Oh, leave me alone. I don't have time to change. I'll be late," she told Nicole.

"We're going to talk about this later," Nicole called after her. Kids! But she soon put aside all thoughts of Mollie. Today was her day!

She waited as patiently as possible for Mark to appear, and when his Chevy pulled into the driveway, she grabbed her purse and jacket and ran for the car.

Slamming the door behind her, she smiled at him, but her happy greeting faltered. He didn't look very well. In fact, he looked positively ill—there were heavy shadows under his brown eyes, which looked more red than brown at the moment.

"Are you okay?"

"Sure," Mark mumbled. "It's just an allergy attack. I already took some medicine."

"But doesn't that make you drowsy?"

"Course not," he mumbled again. "Be fine in an hour or two. Honest."

"I hope so," Nicole said. "Are you sure you feel up to the drive?"

"No sweat." Mark pulled out into the road. "You just read the map."

The journey to Los Angeles was not difficult, but there were several interchanges to cross, and driving required concentration. The traffic was heavy, and Nicole was secretly glad she hadn't attempted to make the trip alone. Hardly had the thought crossed her mind, however, when another glance at Mark revealed his head nodding slightly over the wheel.

"Mark!"

He raised his head quickly, blinking. "Sorry."

"Are you sleepy?"

He nodded, looking sheepish.

"Pull off at the next exit, Mark, and let me drive. It's not safe for you to drive in this condition."

He looked relieved, but as he pulled the car toward the exit ramp, he said, "The traffic's pretty thick. Think you can manage?"

"Of course; I've been driving for over a year," Nicole reminded him, although she didn't feel as confident as she sounded.

After they made the exchange, Nicole headed back into the stream of cars and trucks that lined the freeway. Nicole had mostly driven on local streets, and the constant rush of speeding cars and seemingly giant trucks made the muscles in her neck and shoulders tense as she gripped the wheel tightly. Mark, in the passenger's seat, put on his seat belt and promptly went to sleep.

"Poor baby," Nicole murmured, glancing at him affectionately, then hurriedly transferred her attention back to the road as a long rig threatened to push her out of her lane.

For some time she drove carefully, turning the volume of the radio down so that Mark could sleep undisturbed. But when a freeway interchange loomed ahead, Nicole, in a surge of panic, discovered she'd forgotten which way to go.

"Mark, quick, look at the map," she said urgently.

"What?" Mark tried to focus his eyes.

Nicole had no time to think about it. The cars zoomed along and she had to choose. She steered the car to the left, and sighed.

"Which freeway are we supposed to be on?" she asked.

Mark rubbed his eyes and consulted the map, then studied the signs along the side of the road. "Not this one," he told her.

"Figures," Nicole groaned.

Neither of them was familiar with the L.A. freeway system, and they had to exit, pull over, and consult the map before deciding how to find their way back to the correct route. By the time Nicole finally ended up on Wilshire Boulevard amid heavy downtown traffic and saw the Los Angeles Museum of Art ahead of them, her shoulders were aching with tension and her head throbbed.

But when they parked the car and made their way toward the large building, her elation returned.

"We're really here!" She grabbed Mark's arm, and her excitement was contagious. He grinned down at her.

"Sure."

"How do you feel?"

"Better." He looked much more alert. Nicole, thankful that she wouldn't have to make the drive back, forgot everything except the exhibit.

It was in a special section of the museum, and after they bought their tickets, they had to stand in line for half an hour to see the popular exhibition. But when Nicole was finally allowed through the doors, she caught her breath.

"Look!"

Mark, whose interest in art was not extensive, simply nodded as Nicole exclaimed over painting after painting, and followed her as she lost herself in a happy daze, wandering from one painting to another.

Monet, Pissarro, Renoir, Cézanne. Their masterpieces had been collected from all over the world, and Nicole was entranced and captivated by the subtle colors, muted shadows, and dancing lights, by the portraits, still lifes, and landscapes.

Mark, observing her blissful expression, grinned to himself. They were, he admitted, pretty paintings. But he suspected that such mild appreciation would only insult Nicole's enthusiasm, so he kept quiet and allowed her to wander through the rooms in a joyful daze.

Only once, inspecting a collection of paintings done of the same haystacks in different lights and seasons, he murmured, "Couldn't he get it right the first time?"

When he finally persuaded Nicole that it was time to go, leaving barely enough time to buy a souvenir book of prints in the museum shop and grab a quick sandwich in the nearby snack bar, Mark asked, "Was it worth all the hassle?"

"Oh, yes!" Nicole told him. The light in her blue eyes was enough to convince even the most un-artistic observer. Mark squeezed her hand under the table and finished his ham and cheese.

Mark, to Nicole's relief, felt capable of driving home, and they started out without incident. They were soon packed on the freeways with the hordes of city workers now released from work, trying to make their daily commute home.

The stream of traffic, thickened by increasing numbers of cars, slowed until they were hardly moving.

"What a mess," Nicole said. "Mark, you're a doll to go through all this just for me."

"I'm glad we did it," Mark said. "Though I'd hate to make this trip every day."

The cars ahead of them began to pick up speed, and Mark touched the gas pedal. Their car accelerated in rhythm with the long line of traffic.

"Thank goodness," Nicole breathed. "Maybe we

can make some time now." The sun was low in the sky and she thought about Cindy and Mollie. They would have expected her back hours ago.

Then brake lights flickered ahead of them, and Mark reached hastily for the brake.

Nicole held her breath. They skidded to a stop just in time to avoid the big van ahead of them. But just as she was about to relax, a sudden jolt threw them both hard against the restraining seat belts. The truck behind them hadn't been able to stop in time.

"Oh, Mark," Nicole cried, visions of a crumbled car in her mind. She shut her eyes, afraid to look.

Mark, a worried expression on his face, unbuckled his seat belt, turned off the engine, and climbed out to walk back and inspect the damage.

Nicole stayed where she was. The sight of Mark's car, destroyed because he had been nice enough to drive her to the exhibit, was more than she could bear.

For several nerve-racking moments she waited, hearing occasional words as Mark and the truck driver conferred. At least, she thought, no one was shouting.

Finally Mark came back to sit down behind the wheel. "It's okay, just crumpled the fender a little. The poor old car won't notice the difference," he assured her. "The truck isn't damaged at all."

"Thank heavens," Nicole said. "Mark, I'm really sorry about your car."

"It could have happened anywhere," Mark reassured her.

"What do you think is holding up the traffic?" Nicole asked, looking at the cars and trucks that sat motionless in seemingly endless lines.

"The truck driver said he heard on his C.B. radio that there's a big pileup a mile or so ahead. We'll just have to wait for the C.H.P. to sort it out and clear the road."

They looked at each other and grinned.

"Wish I had a soft drink," Mark admitted.

"Wish I had a bathroom." Nicole's comment was rueful.

Mark chuckled. "Can't help you there."

They rolled down the windows of the car, hoping for a slight breeze to ease the waves of heat rising from the sun-warmed asphalt, and settled down to wait.

Mollie kept jumping up from the table to peer out the windows into the dark. She walked over to the kitchen table, where Cindy was sitting, bopping her head and tapping her feet to the tune on her portable stereo. Mollie shouted at her sister, "Do you think they've had a wreck?"

"Be quiet," Cindy told her, removing the headphones. "I don't want to think about it."

"But it's past nine; the museum closed hours ago."

"Maybe they went out for dinner." Cindy tried to be reasonable.

"She didn't say anything about that."

"Maybe they decided at the last minute."

Mollie watched her sister dip into a carton of mint chocolate chip ice cream from the freezer. "How can you eat? Maybe we should call the hospital."

"Which one? L.A. has dozens, maybe hundreds." Cindy licked her spoon.

"Aren't you even worried?" Mollie sounded exasperated, watching Cindy calmly eating her ice cream.

"I'm *trying* not to think about it," Cindy said.

"But it's not fair; I had to worry last time about you, and now it's Nicole!" Mollie's voice rose.

Cindy held out a spoonful of ice cream for her sister. "Take it easy. She's okay."

"How do you know?" Mollie accepted the ice cream, but her tone was still doubtful.

"How do you know she's not?" Cindy, the eternal optimist, pointed out.

Mollie stamped her foot. "Just because you don't care—"

The sound of a car in the driveway stopped the incipient argument, and both girls ran to the window.

"It's Mark's car, I think." Cindy peered into the darkness.

Mollie ran to open the door. Sure enough, there was Nicole coming up the path.

"Where have you been?" Mollie demanded, as her older sister came into the house.

Nicole looked at her in surprise. "You know where I went."

"But what made you so late?"

"We had to sit for hours in a big traffic jam."

"We thought you were in an accident." Mollie didn't seem appeased.

"*You* were the worrywart, shrimp," Cindy corrected. "Not me."

"Actually, we *were* in an accident." Nicole's answer even made Cindy look concerned until she added, "But nothing serious."

"Were you hurt?" Mollie still looked worried.

"Not a bit. Just a creased fender. To the car," she added. "Have you two eaten?"

Mollie nodded. "Cindy heated some soup."

"Good. I'm going to make myself a sandwich and go to bed. I'm exhausted."

"Serves you right; next time don't be so late. Or call," Mollie scolded. The irony of the exchange of roles made Nicole and Cindy laugh, until finally even Mollie saw the humor and grinned reluctantly.

"Go to bed, shrimp," Cindy told her affectionately. "No more disasters this week."

"Good!" Mollie said.

Chapter 9

*W*ednesday morning Nicole went into Mollie's room while Mollie was still dressing for school, and peered over her little sister's shoulder, shaking her head at the high heels, heavy makeup, and snug sweater.

"What are you trying to do, Mollie? Convince the whole freshman class that your ambition in life is to become a lady of the night?"

Mollie's reply was indignant. "It's the style, Nicole. Don't you know anything?" She gestured toward the posters on her wall. Nicole studied the rock stars, with their outrageous outfits and exaggerated makeup and hairstyles.

"Mollie, in the entertainment world people like to look strange to draw attention to themselves. That doesn't mean that you should copy them in real life. This isn't you."

Mollie frowned. "How do you know?"

"Just be yourself, Mollie, and cut out the playacting."

Mollie hesitated, wanting to tell Nicole about her troubles at school. But Nicole, seeing her younger sister's usual stubborn expression, gave up. If Mollie didn't want her advice, that was her problem. "Don't be late," she said, and left the room.

And Mollie, disappointed, thought, She doesn't care enough to listen.

But Nicole's words did leave an impression. Despite Mollie's longing to be considered as mature as her sisters, she was aware, deep down, that Nicole had an irritating habit of being right. So she went to the bathroom, washed her face, and started over with more restraint.

She discarded the sweater for a pink button-down shirt and her shoes for a pair of pink high-top sneakers. Maybe her attempt at high fashion hadn't quite succeeded after all. At least she *felt* more comfortable now.

Later, on her way to French class, she observed Sarah and Linda, their heads together as they whispered in the hall. Talking about her, Mollie guessed from their frequent glances. Alone as usual, she turned toward the classroom and, as the two girls went ahead of her, saw a slip of paper fall from Sarah's notebook.

Mollie picked it up and followed Sarah to her desk. "You dropped something."

Sarah accepted the slip of paper, nodding stiffly.

Both girls seemed to be watching Mollie curiously. Sarah simply stared, but Linda blurted out, "What happened to you today? Run out of makeup?"

Mollie flushed. "I thought I'd try something new, starting high school and all. But I decided it wasn't my style."

"You look like an ordinary person today," Linda said.

"I *am* an ordinary person; what did you think?" Mollie asked, feeling her temper start to rise.

"Well, all that talk about art and culture. We thought you were . . . well, a bit affected."

Mollie cooled down and shrugged. After all, they were right; she hadn't been herself. "I know. I wanted to sound like my older sister. She really does like all that. Me, I'd just as soon watch the latest videos."

"Me, too." Linda grinned. "That's what we're doing after school, at my house. Want to come?"

Mollie glanced at Sarah, whose silent antagonism appeared unabated. "I don't want to cause any problems."

"You seem to do that without trying." Sarah flushed, and then said quickly, "Before you appeared, Tony liked *me*."

"I didn't know he was your boyfriend," Mollie said, glancing toward the dark-haired boy who'd been such a pest. No wonder Sarah had been ready to dislike her.

"I heard he was going to ask you to the game," Sarah said, adding, "Not that I care, of course."

"If he does, I'll say no," Mollie told them. "He's really—" She was about to say "boring," then decided that wasn't too tactful. "—not my type."

"Are you sure?" Sarah brightened up at once.

"Positive."

The sulky expression on Sarah's face disappeared. "I guess I got a bit mad—sorry." She grinned.

Remembering their exchange of insults in French, Mollie giggled. It all seemed funny now. "That's okay, I guess. I really deserved it—I mean, I was pretty nasty myself," Mollie told her.

"If you want to eat lunch with us, we can plan for after school," Sarah said. The two girls smiled at each other.

Mollie felt a great weight lift, and her heart soared until she almost felt she could fly. "I'd love to."

When Cindy got home after practice, she found Nicole in the kitchen, making a salad.

Heading straight for the refrigerator, she asked, "Anything to eat besides rabbit food?"

"There's beef stew in the crock pot."

"Great." Cindy sniffed the air appreciatively. "Where's Mollie?"

"At a friend's house." Then, realizing that Cindy was gobbling down a huge slice of cheese, she almost said something about Cindy spoiling her appetite, but decided to let the matter drop.

"Do you realize"—Nicole frowned at the tomatoes she'd sliced—"that Mom and Dad will be home Saturday?"

"Gosh, what happened to our ten days?"

"What happened to our good times?" Nicole's tone was sharp. "All we've had is one disaster after another!"

"You can say that again!" Cindy agreed.

Nicole looked thoughtful. "I think we deserve at least one evening of fun. Let's have a party Friday night. Nothing fancy—just a few friends. But it's our last night on our own."

"Awesome—a party!" Cindy's green eyes lit up with pleasure. "How many people can I ask?"

"Not the whole polo team," Nicole told her hastily. "Let's keep this manageable, *s'il vous plait.*"

They were still discussing their party when Mollie got home. But Mollie's good mood evaporated when she found that she was to have little voice in the decision-making.

"What about *my* friends."

"You can ask one or two," Nicole told her. "But we've already got more people than we can handle."

"This isn't a kindergarten party," Cindy added.

Mollie sniffed. "Thanks a bunch."

But Nicole and Cindy were too absorbed in their planning to pay attention.

On Thursday, Mollie was disappointed to learn that Sarah and Linda were leaving after school Friday on a camping trip with Sarah's parents and couldn't come to the Lewis sisters' party.

She wasn't sure about inviting Brett. Despite his occasional attentions, she still found it hard to believe that he would really consider going out with a mere freshman. So she approached the subject with considerable caution during speech class.

"We're having a few people over tomorrow night," she told Brett.

"We?"

"My sisters and I—my parents are out of town."

Brett gave an appreciative whistle, which made the teacher glance his way, frowning. "Out of sight! Should be a wild party."

"I don't know about that." Mollie's tone was doubtful. "But if ... if you don't have plans already ..."

He took the ball out of her court with practiced ease. "Is this an invitation? I'm honored." His wide grin and slightly wicked wink made Mollie's heart beat faster. He was really going to come— unbelievable!

Meanwhile, Angela had agreed to come, and Nicole's happiness was complete. Or almost.

"If that girl comes, you're asking for trouble," Bitsy told Nicole during study hall.

"Why?" Nicole, always charitable in her valuations of her friends, stared at Bitsy in real surprise.

"I heard what she and her boyfriend did at the ball game last weekend. He was totally drunk, and she wasn't much better. They sprayed white paint on the other team's bus. If the police knew who did it—"

"I don't believe that." Nicole's voice sharpened in anger. "Angela wouldn't do anything like that. You're just repeating gossip."

"Pardon me," the other girl said, and withdrew behind her textbook.

Nicole sighed. Why did everyone dislike Angela so much?

But she refused to allow anything to destroy her anticipation of Friday night. Nicole, who had visions of becoming as adept a hostess as her mother, took special pleasure in making her plans for the party. She pored through her mother's recipe books for appetizers and dips and spent the last of the grocery money stocking up on soft drinks. Absolutely nothing would ruin this last evening, she vowed privately.

After school on Friday, Nicole and Cindy worked hard preparing for the party, and Mollie did her part without resentment, even when Nicole seemed to give her all the fussy jobs, like dusting the crystal or polishing the silver candlesticks. Mollie drifted through her chores, dreaming of Brett's charming smile. A real date—with a boy as good-looking and mature as Nicole's own friends. What a thought!

After the house had been cleaned and polished to an exemplary degree, and Nicole had finished her preparations in the kitchen, all three girls went upstairs to dress, with only a mild argument over who got the bathroom first. Cindy emerged first, wearing white jeans and, a concession to the special occasion, a yellow blouse instead of her usual sweat shirt.

Mollie, forced as usual to wait for the last turn, took a tepid shower, singing as she shampooed her long hair. She dried her hair with special care, using her curling iron to coax additional curls in the dark waves.

She selected her new lace-trimmed blouse and plaid skirt, put on as much makeup as she dared under Nicole's watchful eye, and waited for the party to start, with a rapid pulse and a multitude of butterflies in her stomach.

The first to arrive were Cindy's crowd: Anna, Duffy, Carey, Randy, and the rest. Although they were fifteen minutes early, they took one look at the carefully prepared house and then attacked the table of food with enthusiasm.

Mark rang the doorbell promptly at seven, and Bitsy and her boyfriend, Jamie, followed soon after. Several other of Nicole's friends arrived.

Mollie, who had been watching the door, jumped every time the doorbell pealed, until finally, when she answered the door for yet another of Nicole's friends, she saw the tall, familiar form sauntering up the walkway.

"Brett!" Her excitement was impossible to conceal.

Flattered by her obvious admiration, Brett

reached forward to crumple one of her carefully groomed curls. "Hi there, pixie."

Mollie, not minding the destruction of her hairstyle in such a good cause, flushed with pleasure. Brett's own special name for her—how exciting!

"I'm so glad you came," Mollie said as they walked inside together. She didn't realize that her shining eyes and flushed cheeks made her feelings obvious, but Brett just grinned.

"Would you like something to drink?"

"Sounds great. Got anything with a kick to it?"

Mollie, her smile becoming a little uncertain, didn't know what to answer. Was he kidding? She certainly hoped so. "It's all in here," she said, and led him to the table, covered with an assortment of foods and trays of different soft drinks.

Brett accepted a glass of cola and helped himself to the food.

"Mollie," Nicole called from the kitchen. "Get in here quick!"

Mollie frowned, but she told Brett, "Back in a minute," and hurried toward the kitchen.

"What do you want?"

Nicole, who didn't seem to notice the urgency of Mollie's question, waved toward another platter of food. "Take that out to the table, please, and then come back and open some more drinks."

Mollie, sighing, did what she was told. After she set the platter carefully on the dining room table and removed an empty plate, she saw that Brett had wandered over to a group of Nicole's friends and seemed to have become part of their laughing crowd.

"But he's *my* friend," Mollie wanted to yell. Instead, she bit back her protest and returned to the kitchen.

It seemed to the impatient Mollie that a hostess's chores were never done—even when there were three hostesses to share them.

"I don't see why I have to do all the work, when I couldn't even invite all the people I wanted to," she grumbled.

But Nicole turned a deaf ear. "Hurry up with those vegetables," she commanded as she whipped up a fresh bowl of dip.

When Mollie finally managed to escape from the kitchen, she found Brett at the other side of the room, talking to one of Nicole's girl friends.

Mollie felt a pang of jealousy. Had Brett forgotten her already? Several couples were dancing to the Rolling Stones song blasting from the stereo. When the girl beside Brett was taken out to dance by another boy, Mollie thought, This is my chance.

Regaining her courage, she walked across the living room to Brett, who grinned at her. Mollie, who thought that being in Brett's arms would be the culmination of a perfect evening, hoped that he would ask her to dance. But when Brett spoke, his thoughts were in a different direction.

"Don't want to put down your little get-together, pixie, but this party is kind of dull, don't you think?"

Mollie, who had been very pleased with their party until now, hastened to agree. "I guess so." To someone like Brett, she told herself, this must be boring indeed. He probably went to more exciting parties every weekend.

As if in confirmation, he lowered his voice and said, "Some of the guys from UCSB are having a *real* party tonight at their apartment. Want to cruise by with me and check it out?"

Mollie hesitated. What would Nicole say? She knew darn well what Nicole would say—"No way." But Mollie was tired to being treated like some junior-grade Cinderella, always in the kitchen when she wanted to be on the dance floor.

"Well . . ." she hesitated.

Across the room, Nicole noticed Mollie in conversation with a boy who was definitely too old for her little sister, but she was too preoccupied to give the matter much thought. Still absorbed in her hostess's duties, she hovered around the table, checking everything one last time, then glanced around the room. The party seemed to be going well: The tapes on the stereo blared; everyone loved the food. Nicole decided that it was time to enjoy her own party. She joined Bitsy and Jamie at the end of the long sofa.

"Great idea, Nicole," Bitsy told her. "Your parents won't mind, will they?"

Nicole smiled. "They trust me."

"I love that green dip." Jamie had no worries to spoil his attention to the food. "Is there any more?"

Nicole jumped up again. "I'll get some."

She brought out another bowl of dip, added more vegetables and chips to the trays, then allowed Mark to persuade her to dance to the dreamy tune on the stereo.

As Mark held her close, Nicole laid her cheek against his shoulder and whispered, "Do you think the party is a success?"

"Perfect!"

Nicole felt a surge of pride and relief. But what had happened to Angela?

The peal of the doorbell, cutting through the last of the song, seemed to answer her question. Nicole stepped reluctantly out of Mark's embrace and hurried to the door.

Angela stood in the doorway, looking very elegant and overdressed in tight black pants and a sequined top. A tall, stocky boy stood behind her.

"Hi, Nicole." Angela came into the hallway. "This is Dan."

Nicole, glancing at Angela's outfit, greeted them both. Surely she had warned Angela that the party was informal. But maybe this was the custom back east. Who was she to tell Angela what to wear?

"Everyone else is already here; come on in."

Afterward, Nicole would chart the downfall of the party from the moment when Angela walked into the room. Bitsy and Jamie and two other couples were dancing. Cindy and her group, and apparently Mollie as well, had gone to the family room.

Angela paused at the entrance to the living room, put her hands on her hips, and sniffed. She didn't seem impressed.

"Come on, let's dance," she told her grinning boyfriend.

Dan seemed rather unsteady on his feet, but Angela hardly needed a partner. No doubt about it, she was an accomplished dancer, Nicole thought, but her one-woman exhibition was a bit much. Bitsy and the other kids walked through the archway into the dining room to the table of food, talking quietly among themselves.

When the song ended, Angela shook her mop of hair and seemed to notice for the first time that they were alone.

"I can see this isn't going to be much fun," she told her burly boyfriend, who hardly seemed capable of speech.

Angela didn't bother to lower her voice, and Nicole winced. Why was Angela being deliberately antagonistic?

"Wouldn't you like something to eat?" Nicole tried to rescue the situation.

Cindy and her group of friends reappeared in the doorway just in time to see Dan pick up a cracker and sample the dip. "Not bad," he said.

Cindy, walking past Dan, made a face. "Nicole," she whispered to her sister, "he smells like a brewery!"

"Oh, no." Nicole bit her lip. "No wonder he looks so unsteady."

They watched as Dan picked up a glass of cola and managed to get the glass safely to his lips.

"Angela," Nicole said quietly, "don't you think you should drive Dan home? He can hardly stand up."

"Don't be a prude." Angela only grinned. "Dan's okay. You worry too much, Nicole."

"Somebody talking about me?" Dan turned awkwardly toward them, and the liquid in the glass sloshed just as Bitsy and Jamie walked up to the table. The cola splashed Bitsy's white blouse.

"Now look what you've done!" Bitsy gasped.

"You got in my way," Dan said.

Jamie's expression became belligerent. "You've got the manners of a warthog, you know that?"

"Hey, it's no b-big deal." Dan's words were slightly slurred.

Nicole, completely disgusted, glared at him. How could Angela have brought Dan to their party in this condition?

But Jamie's reaction was more graphic. "You think so? You have some, then." He picked up a glass of cola and dashed the contents into Dan's face.

While Dan sputtered in surprise, Angela shrieked, "You rat!" She grabbed a piece of pizza and tossed it toward Jamie. It hit him square in the face.

Jamie yelped, then shook his head. The mistreated piece of pizza fell to the floor, leaving his face covered with tomato sauce and cheese, and a slice of pepperoni adhering to his nose.

Cindy laughed despite herself.

Nicole threw her sister an angry glance, then turned to Angela. "Angela, I think—"

But Angela didn't seem to hear. She picked up a handful of chips covered with cheese sauce and advanced toward Jamie.

"Angela—"

Jamie, one eye shut as he tried to focus on the pepperoni that seemed to have sprouted from his nose, didn't notice her approach. But when Angela pulled the collar of his V-neck knit shirt forward and dumped the sticky food down his chest, he let out a howl.

Grabbing some fruit slices from the table, he threw them, but his aim was wild. Cindy ducked, but Anna was too slow. A piece of pear and two grapes caught in her hair. "Hey!"

"Food fight!" Dan yelled gleefully.

"Bitsy, stop him," Nicole begged as Jamie turned to the table for more food. Bitsy ran up to her boyfriend just as Angela caught up another piece of pizza and Dan grabbed a bowl of onion dip.

"Jamie—" Bitsy began, when Angela's toss caught her by surprise. The pizza grazed her cheek, dropping bits of red tomato sauce over her already stained blouse. Bitsy's bewildered expression quickly changed to one of pure rage.

"Enough, already!" she cried, and grabbed a large bowl of guacamole dip.

Nicole gasped. "Bitsy, no!"

The green gunk hit Angela on the side of the face, and dip spattered Cindy and half the room at the same time as Dan's onion dip landed on Cindy's friend Carey.

Cindy, rubbing a dab off her chin, stuck her finger into her mouth. "Needs more chili powder, Nicole."

But Anna and Carey, enraged, turned to the nearest bowls of food, while Nicole ran from one friend to another.

"Cindy, help me!"

Cindy tried to grab Anna's arm, causing her to lose control of her handful of food.

Duffy, receiving a bit of cauliflower complete with sour cream in the eye, blinked and wiped away the sticky cream.

"You asked for it!" he said as he searched the table for food.

Cindy started to yell at him, but just then an olive flew into her open mouth. She choked and sputtered.

Nicole, shocked speechless by the sight of food flying through her once immaculate house, pounded her sister on the back.

Cindy, her eyes watering and her face red from coughing, finally was able to speak. "I'm all right."

Able to turn away from her sister, Nicole grabbed Duffy, who reluctantly lowered his handful of chips. But by now everyone was into the act and food was still flying through the air until Nicole finally jumped onto a chair, yelling, "Stop!"

Anna put down a piece of pizza. Carey returned a handful of shrimp to the table. Jamie and Mark, in the midst of belting Dan with chocolate sauce, stopped.

Bitsy, who was chasing Angela around the coffee table, trying to drop a piece of cake down her low-cut top, didn't appear to hear. Nicole charged after her best friend, then decided that this was ridiculous. Stopping, she caught her tiny friend on the next go-round, putting her arms bodily around her. "Bitsy, stop!"

Angela's wails subsided. Dan, barely conscious by now, leaned across one of the dining chairs, chocolate sauce dripping down his nose.

"I think you'd better leave." Nicole made her voice as stern as she knew how. She looked at Angela as if she'd never seen her before.

"If Dan goes, I go too," Angela sulked.

"That's exactly what I had in mind," Nicole assured her. "Mark, help that ... that bozo out of here."

When the door shut behind the two, Nicole and Cindy surveyed the havoc of their home, dismay plain on both faces.

As Nicole tried to pick up the fern that had been dislodged from its pot, Bitsy came over. "Nicole, I'm sorry. We'll help you clean this up."

Nicole, though visibly touched, shook her head. "It's not your fault. Angela and Dan started it. I should have seen through Angela before. All her rudeness couldn't have come from homesickness; I should have known that. Cindy and I will take care of the mess."

But the zest had disappeared from the party, and the rest of the kids soon departed. Mark offered to stay and help, but Nicole, determined not to make any of her friends suffer for her mistake, refused his help.

"Want to send me away, too?" Cindy asked hopefully, looking over the wrecked house.

"Nope, this party was half yours, and your friends had the best aim," Nicole reminded her sister. "You can help clean up. After you get the guacamole out of your hair. I didn't mean this to happen, though."

"That's the breaks." Cindy shrugged as she gingerly put her hand to her head. "Doesn't Mollie get a share in the dirty work?"

"She's gone to bed already, I guess," Nicole said absently. "Oh, no!"

"What's wrong now?"

"Mother's crystal animals—someone's knocked them out of the shadow box. Help me. If any of these are broken, I'll shoot myself!"

Nicole, on her hands and knees, felt through the thick carpet for each tiny piece of crystal. Cindy hurried to help her. One after another of the small objects was retrieved and placed carefully back into its rightful position. At last only one piece was still missing.

"The unicorn—that's Mom's favorite," Cindy worried. "She'll notice it missing right away."

Nicole, who needed no reminder, put one hand to her face. "Where can it be? If it had broken, at least we'd find the pieces."

"You don't think Angela could have taken it, do you?"

"You mean stolen it? I'm sure she's not a thief!"

"I bet you didn't think she started food fights, either," Cindy argued. "If not her, then that goon of a boyfriend. He looked capable of anything."

Nicole, remembering his beery breath, shuddered. "What are we going to do?"

"If Mom and Dad find out—" Worry clouded Cindy's usually carefree expression.

"Don't even think that," Nicole begged. "Where did Mom buy that unicorn? Maybe we can replace it."

"At that glass shop in the mall. Do you think it's still open?" Cindy glanced toward the wall clock, only to discover the dial was obscured by guacamole.

"Friday they're open late. We've got thirty minutes!"

"Do you have any money?" Cindy asked. "I'm broke."

"Mother left me one of her credit cards; I'll have to pay her back later. If only she doesn't discover we lost her unicorn."

"What about Mollie?" Cindy asked as Nicole ran to get her purse.

"Go tell her what's happening, or she may get frightened if she wakes and finds we're not here," Nicole ordered. "Hurry!"

Cindy ran up the stairs, but she came down even faster a moment later.

"Mollie's gone!"

Chapter 10

"What do you mean, Mollie's gone?" Nicole stared at Cindy, unable to accept her blunt declaration.

"She's gone; she's not in bed."

"Did you check the bathroom?"

"I'm not stupid," Cindy retorted.

"Look in the family room; maybe she decided to watch television awhile."

Cindy looked doubtful, but she did as she was told. Meanwhile, Nicole went to the kitchen, hoping to find Mollie sitting at the table with a late-night snack. But the kitchen was empty, and when Cindy returned, one glance told Nicole that she had had the same result.

"Where could she be?"

Cindy shrugged. Nicole felt a stirring panic and tried to control her fear. "Maybe she went over to see a friend. Do you know Arlene's number?"

Cindy shook her head. "But Mollie's phone book is on her bedside table."

"Go get it."

When Cindy came back with the small pink book, Nicole flipped through the pages until she found Arlene's number. Using the kitchen phone, she dialed the number, while Cindy stood beside her, her expression worried.

"Arlene? Is Mollie at your house?"

Cindy held her breath.

"Oh." The disappointment in Nicole's tone left no doubt as to Arlene's answer. "She didn't call you tonight? Thanks anyhow."

"Now what?" Cindy asked.

"What's the name of the girl in Mollie's French class that she went home with after school?"

"Sallie . . . no, Sarah." Cindy thought hard.

Nicole went through the phone book again and tried this number. She held the receiver tightly and both girls could hear the thin ringing, but there was no answer.

"I think she was going out of town this weekend," Cindy remembered. An awful thought had been gnawing at the edge of her mind, and Cindy added with a rush, "You don't think she's run away, do you?"

The idea of Mollie alone at night in some strange place made Nicole's head spin. "She wouldn't be so foolish . . . I think."

"We weren't very nice to her about the party," Cindy pointed out. Her usually carefree grin had disappeared, and her green eyes were wide with worry.

"We haven't been very nice to her for two weeks, if you want to know the truth." Nicole bit her lip. "We haven't paid very much attention to her, either. I hope she's okay."

"If she is, I won't yell at her for at least a week!" Cindy promised.

"If she's just okay"—Nicole took a deep breath—"I'll probably strangle her for pulling such a stunt!"

Cindy, despite her worry, grinned briefly.

"Wait a minute!" Nicole said.

"What is it?"

"That blond boy she was talking to at the party—who was he?"

"I don't know," Cindy said. "I thought you invited him; I think he's a senior."

"He *is* a senior, but I can't remember his name. I thought you invited him; Mollie must have."

"What's Mollie doing hanging around with a senior?" Cindy sounded nonplussed.

Nicole shook her head, trying to think.

"I told you Vista High wasn't ready for Mollie," Cindy continued darkly. "A senior, yet."

"Maybe they went somewhere together."

"Brilliant deduction, Sherlock."

"Let's drive down and check out Taco Rico and the pizzeria." Nicole reached once more for her purse and the keys to the family station wagon.

That reminded Cindy of their earlier emergency. "What about the unicorn, Nicole?"

Nicole groaned. "I don't know, but we've got to find Mollie first. Mom will be furious if we've lost her unicorn, but she'll kill us if we've lost Mollie!"

The two girls ran for the garage, where what appeared to be a black bear but was only Winston, confined to the garage for the duration of the party, bounded happily up to greet them.

"No, Winston." Cindy tried to push the big dog back. "You can't go."

Nicole, peering into the darkness, which suddenly looked unfriendly, said, "Let him come."

So they allowed Winston to lie down in his accustomed position in the back of the station wagon, and Nicole carefully backed out of the garage and turned into the street.

When they left the party together, Mollie followed Brett out to the curb to his parked car, a long, sleek red Corvette.

"Like it?" Brett's tone was proud.

"It's awesome," Mollie said, borrowing Cindy's favorite expression. "What a car!"

As Brett opened the door for her, Mollie was even happier that she had agreed to go. Even Nicole didn't ride around in a car like this, Mollie thought smugly.

During the drive Brett kept up a flow of clever quips that kept Mollie giggling. He drove with both hands on the wheel, and the floorshift sat comfortingly between the two bucket seats. Mollie felt safe and extremely grown-up and sophisticated, and tried to match Brett's jokes with a few of her own.

But when they pulled up in front of a modern apartment building and Mollie stared through the darkness at the uncurtained window where several boys—men?—were outlined against the bright lights, Mollie felt her courage waver. The loud music that floated through the open window was punctuated by waves of laughter, and Mollie could see half-full beer bottles perched on the windowsill.

When she watched one tall figure stand up unsteadily, sloshing the liquid in his glass, Mollie knew instinctively that this party was way beyond her level.

"Brett?" she said as he opened his car door and turned to look at her. "I've changed my mind."

Under his inquiring gaze, Mollie flushed, but held her position stubbornly. "I don't think I'm in the mood for a party tonight. Do you mind?"

He frowned, but almost at once his expression lightened. "Sure. You'd rather we were alone; is that it?"

"Yes." Mollie nodded, eager for any way out of this embarrassing situation.

"Why didn't you say so, pixie?" Brett's good humor had miraculously returned.

He shut his door again and flipped the key in the ignition. As the engine roared, he said over the noise, "I know this little canyon—"

Panicked once more at the thought of being lost on some winding back road with a boy whom—she had just begun to realize—she hardly knew, Mollie spoke quickly. "Why don't we drive down by the beach? It's awfully romantic at night."

Brett grinned, a knowing look in his eye. "Sure thing, pixie."

As he turned the car back toward the beach, Mollie tried to relax. Watching the bright neon lights on stores and restaurants flash by the moving car, she felt a spark of excitement glow inside her.

"This is unbelievable," she said, half to herself, "being out at night—" before she added, "just like a real date."

Brett grinned at this exhibition of naïveté. "You haven't been around much, have you, pixie?"

Flustered—she didn't want Brett to think she was a baby—Mollie tried to project an aura of sophistication.

"Sure I have . . . I mean, I just like the city at night, that's all."

"Sure," Brett agreed, trying not to grin.

"Benito's—that's a good restaurant." Mollie spoke a little too wildly as they passed the quiet family restaurant. "Do you like Italian food?" She didn't really know what Brett liked, and the thought only increased her nervousness.

"Not there," Brett told her. "That place is dull;

too many little old ladies and balding business-men."

"Of course," Mollie hastened to agree, afraid she was betraying her lack of experience again. "What do you like to eat?"

"Pizza and a mug of beer," Brett told her. "Of course, I like sweet things, too."

Mollie had the uneasy feeling he didn't mean food. "That's nice," she murmured, swallowing hard.

They were in sight of the beach now, and Mollie directed him toward her favorite lookout point.

"Are you a beach bum?" she asked, adding hastily, "I mean, do you like to surf?"

"Not my thing, pixie," Brett told her. "Too much effort involved."

"Oh." Mollie nodded. "My sister Cindy's a great surfer. She's better than most of the boys at school."

"Bet that makes her popular."

"What?" Something in his tone made Mollie's eyes widen.

"Well, there are times and places for girls, you know. Taking all the glory away from the guys isn't what girls are supposed to do."

"Why not?" Mollie's indignation suddenly rose at this insulting remark. "She's good—why should she hide it?"

"Okay, already." Brett's tone was soothing.

"Now, my oldest sister, Nicole—she likes to

cook and draw and design. That's what she's good at. Me, I'm not too sure what I'm good at yet."

"We haven't covered your grandmother yet, or your canary."

"What? I don't have a canary." Confused, Mollie stared at him.

"I mean, there are better things to do at the beach than discuss your sisters."

Mollie gripped her hands tightly together in her lap. "Oh." She looked through the windows of the car. The sand was silvered by occasional touches of moonlight, and the pale glint of the car's head-lights defied the first faint tendrils of fog.

"Want to go skinny-dipping?"

Mollie stared at Brett in horror. Surely he was joking. But she had to say something. "Wouldn't it be awfully cold?" she finally ventured.

Brett's shout of laughter made her jump again. "Pixie, you're a scream!"

Again, Mollie didn't know what to answer. So she just smiled at him, trying not to reveal the small tornadoes that whirled inside her midsection. They sat in silence, listening to the waves lap against the beach.

Brett reached across the gearshift and pulled her into a practiced embrace. Mollie, her heart beating wildly, felt that she was floating. Trying to relax in his arms, she could smell the spicy scent of his cologne. She started to relax.

But then he leaned forward, while his face moved

closer to hers, and Mollie, overcome by a sudden burst of panic, sat upright with a jerk.

Brett looked confused. "What's wrong?"

Mollie sat perfectly still, scarlet with embarrassment.

"Isn't that what you wanted?" Brett stared at her through the darkness, illuminated only by the faint reflection from the headlights.

"What made you think that?" Mollie asked shrilly, and Brett drew back into his own seat.

"You were the one who said you wanted to be alone with me," he pointed out, his tone a mixture of injured pride and annoyance.

"I didn't mean *that* alone." Mollie suddenly got angry at his annoyed tone.

"Great way to treat a guy," Brett grumbled.

"I'll give you a handkerchief to cry on," Mollie snapped. "But first you can take me home!"

"Fine with me!" Brett agreed, and turned the key in the ignition. But this time, instead of a muffled roar, they heard only a faint clicking.

"Oh, no," Brett groaned. "My battery again; I shouldn't have left the blasted lights on!"

Releasing the hood latch, he climbed out of the low-slung sports car to lift the hood and peer underneath, as if he could by sheer concentration recharge his weakened battery.

Mollie stayed in her bucket seat, and her thoughts were as dark as the drifting fog outside, now beginning to thicken.

What a spot to be stranded in! How would they

get home? The thought of walking home in the dark made her shiver. Brett wouldn't go off and leave her, would he?

She made a fervent promise to herself that she would never again go off alone with a boy whom she hardly knew. Gripping her hands together in her lap, Mollie berated herself aloud.

"You dummy, it's your own fault. You must have marshmallows for brains!"

Then, out of the fog-laced darkness, a massive form appeared with an abruptness that made Mollie gasp. The hapless Brett, tossed against the front of the car by this charging demon, yelled in terror.

While Mollie tried to make out what was happening, she heard the scrape of shoe leather against metal as Brett scrambled to safety atop the small car.

"Get away from me!" he shouted.

Chapter 11

"*W*inston!" *a familiar voice called through* the darkness. "Come here."

"Nicole!" Mollie tumbled out of the car, forgetting everything except her joy at the sight of her sister.

Winston rushed up to her, licking her face, and Mollie hugged the big shaggy head, then gently pushed him away.

"Down, boy," she ordered, and the dog, his heavy tail thumping against the side of the car, calmed his expressions of devotion.

"What *is* that thing?" a male voice demanded. Mollie and Nicole, and then Cindy, all looked up to see Brett sprawled across the roof of his car. "A bear?"

Mollie began to giggle, and the other girls, unable to resist the humor of the situation, joined in while Brett, his red face hidden by the darkness, slid off the roof of the car, nothing damaged except his pride.

Nicole put her arm around Mollie. "Mollie, we're going to murder you, but I'm glad you're all right."

"We looked all over," Cindy told Mollie. "Then I remembered this spot was one of your favorites."

"I'm fine—honest," Mollie reassured them.

Nicole shook her head. "We can see that now."

Cindy added, "Pretty stupid thing to do, shrimp."

Mollie bit her lip, looking so contrite that Nicole's anger faded. "Don't ever go off like that again without telling us."

"I won't," Mollie promised. "But I really felt left out of the party."

Nicole and Cindy looked at each other. "I guess that was our fault," Cindy said. "I'm sorry."

"I'm *très* sorry," Nicole added. "We haven't paid much attention to you lately. We didn't realize. This weekend we'll have a long talk about school, and anything else that's bothering you, okay?"

"Great." The last of Mollie's lingering resentment disappeared, and she felt a rush of affection for her sister. "You already helped me, actually, when you told me to stop playacting and be myself. I don't feel like the Lone Ranger at school anymore, and I've met some nice girls."

"Good. Let's get home; it's cold out here." The girls, followed by Winston, started to walk toward the station wagon.

"Hey," Brett called. "What about me?"

Nicole raised her eyebrows, but Mollie hastened to explain. "His car won't start; the battery is dead."

"Oh," Nicole said. "I don't have any jumper cables; do you?"

Brett shook his head. "Can you drop me off at home? I'll have to get my dad to come back and jump my battery. He's going to murder me," Brett ended glumly, and the girls grinned.

"Sure," Nicole told him.

After a ride complicated by Winston's attempts to climb over the back seat and lick Brett's unwilling face, at last they deposited Brett at his house. Then the girls turned toward home.

"It's too late for the Crystal Shop, I guess," Cindy said.

Nicole nodded. "It closed an hour ago. We're just going to have to tell Mom the truth and hope she'll eventually forgive us."

"Fat chance," Cindy replied glumly.

Mollie opened her eyes wide. "What are you talking about?"

"Mom's crystal unicorn is missing—you didn't notice anyone handling it during the party, did you?"

Mollie shook her head. "That's terrible; that's Mom's favorite piece."

"I know," Nicole agreed sadly. "Still, we might be forgiven for losing the unicorn; we'd have had a hard time explaining how we lost you!"

Mollie blushed and tried to change the subject.

"Did everyone have a good time at the party after I left?"

To her surprise, both girls groaned. "You missed the food fight of the century," Cindy told her.

"You're kidding! In *our* house?"

As the station wagon pulled into the garage, Nicole pushed the automatic garage opener. "Just wait," she told her sister.

In fact, the living room and dining room looked even worse than they remembered.

"There's pizza and dip all over the carpet," said Mollie, who, despite their warning, was aghast at the mess.

"And the tomato sauce has dried," Cindy said. "Let's face it; we'll never get this up, Nicole."

"We have to." Nicole's voice was grim. "Get the carpet cleaner, Cindy. Mollie, you pull out the vacuum. I'll get a pail of water."

Winston, meanwhile, did his part by gobbling up bits of pizza from the floor.

With all three girls scrubbing, the carpet as well as the cushions on the couch eventually came clean, although Nicole was concerned that it wouldn't dry on time. Accordingly, the girls brought down their blow-dryers and took turns directing the warm air toward the carpet.

Then Mollie used glass cleaner on the glass panels of the stereo cabinet and the pictures on the wall, while Cindy and Nicole gathered all the glasses and dishes and took them to the kitchen to wash.

"Why don't we just put them in the dishwasher?" Cindy suggested when Nicole started washing them by hand.

Nicole shook her head. "I don't want Mom to see the evidence."

"Good thinking."

They had almost finished the stack of dirty dishes when Cindy gave a war whoop worthy of Geronimo.

Nicole jumped, and the glass she was washing slipped through her fingers and crashed into the sink, shattering into a dozen pieces.

"Now see what you did!"

Mollie hurried to the kitchen door to see what was amiss, still holding her cleaning rags.

"Forget the glass—look what I found in the bowl of clam dip!" She held aloft a tiny object, its form obscured by the clinging dip.

Nicole stared at it for a moment, then gasped. "The unicorn!"

"How on earth did it get there?" Mollie wondered.

But Nicole, carefully washing the tiny crystal piece in tepid water, said, "Who cares? As long as we found it!"

By the time the Lewis home had been restored to its normal order, the clock on the kitchen wall revealed that Saturday morning had already begun, and the sky outside the window was streaked with the first glimpse of predawn light.

"I've never been so tired in my life," Cindy announced.

Nicole pushed a lock of brown hair back from her eyes and nodded. "Me, too. Every muscle in my body aches. Where's Mollie?"

Cindy went to the doorway and looked through. "Asleep on the couch," she said.

"Wake her up and tell her to go to bed."

"Wow," Cindy said, looking at the time. "We're going to have just enough time to get in bed before it's time to get up!"

The sleepy Mollie, protesting, was persuaded to move toward her bedroom. Cindy and Nicole stood at the bottom of the stairs.

"I don't think I've got enough energy to climb them," Cindy said. "Can I sleep in the garage with Winston?"

Nicole, too weary to answer, simply pointed upstairs, and they climbed the stairs slowly.

When Nicole's alarm went off, she reached blindly for her clock radio, trying to shut off the ringing. But the noise continued, and Nicole opened one eye to stare at the offending alarm. Then she realized it wasn't her alarm at all—she had been so tired she'd forgotten to set it—but the doorbell.

Bounding out of bed, she reached hastily for her robe. "They're home, they're home," she shouted as she headed for the stairs.

Winston barked loudly from the garage as Nicole unlocked and opened the front door. Behind a large stack of packages stood a slim form that Nicole correctly identified as her mother.

"Mom," she cried, hugging her despite her laden arms, causing most of the packages to fall to the porch with a series of muffled thuds.

"Nicole, I missed all of you so much. Everything all right?"

"Of course," Nicole assured her, grateful that she had no disaster to report. "We're fine."

"Sorry I had to wake you, but I couldn't reach my key, and your dad is putting the car into the garage."

"Did you get all of that onto the plane?" Nicole wondered, helping her mother gather up the packages.

Her mother smiled. "It was quite a challenge. Your father threatened to sit in the back and pretend that he didn't know me."

"Tell me all about Japan. Did you have a good time?"

"Wonderful," her mother said. "Wait till you see the kimono I brought you—the most beautiful silk—"

Then Cindy jumped halfway down the stairs, landing with a thump in the front hall. "Mom!" She grabbed her mother in a bear hug, and Mollie was only moments behind.

"Don't I get some of those?"

All three girls turned to see their dad coming in through the kitchen, Winston jumping around him, and there were more hugs for everyone.

While Mr. Lewis carried their bags in from the

car, Mrs. Lewis looked around the living room. "Everything looks spotless, girls."

"Coffee's ready," Nicole called from the kitchen.

Mr. Lewis, about to follow his wife to the breakfast table, almost tripped over a Boston fern, which they had forgotten to put back in the living room. As he returned it to its rightful place, he poked gently into the base.

"New type of plant food, Cindy?" His brown eyes held a quizzical gleam as he held up a small shrimp.

Cindy gulped and hurried out to the kitchen.

While the girls opened the stack of presents their parents had brought, *oh*ing and *ah*ing over the beautiful colors and delicate fabrics, Mrs. Lewis asked, "How's school? Mollie, did you find some old friends?"

"Not really," Mollie told them. "But I made some new ones, I think."

"That's the spirit," her father said. "If you don't get what you want the first time, just jump in there and make it work."

Mollie, remembering her bouts of self-pity the first week, blushed under his words of praise.

"And you two?" Mrs. Lewis asked. "How's school?"

"Fine," Cindy said, and Nicole nodded her agreement.

"You certainly did a good job in the house." Mrs. Lewis smiled at her daughters. Their grins were a bit sheepish. "I'm really proud of the way you've handled the extra responsibilities while we were gone."

"Now wait," Mr. Lewis cautioned. "Before we hand out the medals, I want to hear the real story. There must have been *some* glitches. Confess!"

The three sisters looked at one another.

"I broke a glass," Nicole said, "but it was only second-best."

"I called the fire department," Mollie admitted, "but we put out the fire."

"And I busted my head against the mast of a boat—but not badly," Cindy hastened to add.

Mrs. Lewis, caught with her coffee cup in the air, set it down abruptly and looked at her husband for reassurance. "Good heavens!"

But their father only grinned. "Situation normal, I'd say."

Here's a look at what's in store for you in TOO LATE FOR LOVE, book two in the "Sisters" series for GIRLS ONLY.

"Hi, Grant! I'm Cindy. Cindy Lewis. Welcome to Santa Barbara." But even as she spoke, she surprised herself by thinking that with his incredibly broad shoulders, white teeth, and perfectly even dark tan, Grant McPhearson fit her kid sister Mollie's description of a hunk to a tee.

"Hi, Cindy," Grant said, looking from Cindy to Duffy, who still had his arm slung casually across the blond girl's shoulder. "I hear you're pretty heavily into surfing. I guess I am, too."

"You *guess* you are?" Duffy scoffed, and this time whacked Grant across the shoulder. "MacPhearson, she's super. In fact, at least three of those trophies you saw outside the gym were Cindy's. Including the one for the California statewide women's surfing championship. And she was just fourteen! Plus a couple of those swimming trophies too. You're talking to the apple of Coach Roscoe's eye."

"I believe that!" Grant said. Cindy looked up quickly and met Grant's eyes. He held her glance for a long instant. When she looked away she felt confused and a little bit flattered. Duffy never looked at her like that.

Cindy had rarely seen a surfer look as good as Grant MacPhearson—in more ways than one. Grant's strong muscular body glistened in the spray and sun. Did all surfers from Hawaii look like that? Cindy wondered. Then her hometown pride got rankled. She realized that none of the kids around the local scene were that good. In fact, watching Grant ride a huge wave into shore, Cindy realized he was the first kid her age she'd met who really was better than she was.

"Hey, MacPhearson," Duffy called as he strode up, followed by Joey Marvel and Tom Patnick. "You were out of sight. That was a regular tidal wave you rode in, man. Did you see him, Cindy? He's going to be great for the Surfing Club."

What was the matter with everyone, anyway? Didn't they have any pride? Without saying another word, Cindy tore off her dad's old demin work short, grabbed her surfboard, and ran headlong toward the water.

"Hey, watch it. It's really rough out there," Grant called after Cindy. A look of real concern crossed his face as he turned quickly to Duffy. "I'm not kidding. I almost went under for real beyond the breakers."

"Don't worry," Cindy shouted back over her shoulder as she paused a minute before plunging into the water. "I can take care of myself. "

But her words were lost in the roar of the surf.